Beyond Time and Tide

By

Anna Franklin Osborne

WHAT READERS SAID ABOUT WALKING WOUNDED

The writing style was so powerful, the sorrow and grief are effortlessly displayed. I could not help but feel as though I were part of their family, sharing their strife. The ending was stunning.
Sarah: Trisarahtopsblog.com

I honestly can't remember the last time a book touched me quite as much; it is beautiful, heartbreaking, and real. *Walking Wounded* is beautifully written. One of the only other books I've read that has covered anything even close is *Goodnight, Mr Tom* by Michelle Magorian. I sobbed, I laughed, I loved, and I hated throughout this book, and I cannot wait for more from Anna Franklin Osborne.
Helen Giles: Lifeofanerdishmum.blogspot.co.uk

This made me think about the world we live in and how lucky I am to have the things I have. A highly recommended read and one that will make you think.
Emma Shearer: Lifeliesandalltimecraziness.wordpress.com

This powerful story takes us on a journey through hard to discuss subjects, including domestic abuse and baby loss. Something that many readers may find upsetting, yet the author handles the topics with respect and tenderness. Teenagers will find this a simple read to enjoy after school (especially A-level history students), *Walking Wounded* is a superb book from a brand-new author, it kept me yearning for more and truly made me think about the past and what our country, men, and women all went through together. An excellent book that I shall certainly find myself reading again.
Hazel Newhouse: Thenewhousefamily.co.uk

A stunning debut. This is a very emotional read, a book that has the power to bring you back to a time in our society that should never be forgotten. Reading *Walking Wounded* was like picking up a diary of a survivor…
Mairead O'Driscoll Hearne: Swirlandthread.com

It is such a tragedy for any family to have gone through the horrors of a world war, but for families to have gone through two in their lifetime is just devastating. A fabulous account of a moment in history, highly recommended.
Susan Hampson: booksfromdusktilldawn.wordpress.com

Anna is a wonderful writer. It's hard to believe this is her debut novel. This book had me hooked from the start. I love history and

she brings the characters to life so brilliantly. She beautifully captures the essence of the era, the utter horror that our soldiers must have felt while at war, and the anguish those left behind felt. I cannot recommend this book enough.
Emma Mitchell: emmathelittlebookworm.wordpress.com

I think it's an incredible skill to catch a reader off guard and in the moment, provoking an emotional rollercoaster. This book moved me beyond words. It is a beautiful book, and I can't recommend it highly enough.
Kelly Allen: kellyallenwriter.com

A deeply moving, emotional tale about family, love, and loss during wartime England. The violence and destruction of the war are echoed throughout, but this book isn't just about the war. It is about everyday life, making mistakes, and trying to live with your decisions. But at the heart of it all is a family that loves each other wholeheartedly, no matter what happens, no matter where they are, a secure place to fall when everything else is crumbling around you. This will make you cry and appreciate life, and I highly recommend it to all fiction and historical readers.
Linda Green: Booksofallkinds.weebly.com

A beautifully written, powerful story that had me captivated from the beginning. This has to be one of the best books covering this period that I have read for a long time, and I highly recommend it.

A truly wonderful debut…
Sally Richards

Copyright © Anna Franklin Osborne 2022
First published in 2022 by GooseWing Publications

The right of Anna Franklin Osborne to be identified as the author of the work has been asserted herein in accordance with the Copyright, Designs and Patents Act 1988.

All rights reserved. This book is sold subject to the condition that it shall not, by way of trade or otherwise, be lent, resold, hired out or otherwise circulated without the publisher's prior consent in any form of binding or cover other than that in which it is published and without a similar condition including this condition being imposed on the subsequent purchaser.

All of the characters in this book are fictional but inspired by the lives of real people; and any resemblance to actual people, living or dead, is purely imaginary.

DEDICATION

To my dearest Neil; my husband, my soul mate and my best friend.
You encourage me at every step of the way
and believed in me from the first.
I love you always.

To my children, Emma and Tom, always my greatest fans.
You are my two proudest creations.

PROLOGUE

The day had dawned dry and bright, and a few tourists stood by and watched idly as the little family walked down the ramp.

The old lady paused and reached out for her grandchildren with her wizened hands, and they both reached to steady her as they stepped over the divide to leave the chain ferry.

Every year the same, her rheumy old eyes ignoring the view but sweeping the beach, hardening to gimlets as she focussed on the dog walkers and the day trippers.

Every year since her momentous discovery for Elsie, every year since they were born for them.

But this year was different.

This year they understood why.

And this year would be an end to it.

Part 1

Elsie

CHAPTER 1

An End to Childhood: 1936

It just wasn't fair. Elsie scowled and jabbed the cold sand again with the stick she'd picked up from the driftwood scattered along the high tide mark. She looked out to sea at the little bright sails dotted around the bay and stabbed viciously again, her chestnut hair falling in unruly curls over her eyes.

She'd been so excited when Dad had told her his old friend Robert was coming for the day and bringing his new little boat to take her for a spin in the harbour, or if the weather was good, maybe even out to the open sea. She loved boats and had always longed to sail, but Dad wasn't remotely interested. He might have served in the navy during the Great War but had not been on a boat since, and while she and her brother could both swim like fishes, they'd never once set foot on a boat beyond the little ferry across the River Stour from Christchurch to Wick, a mere two-minute trip, she reflected grimly, stabbing the sand again with the sharp point.

It was the weekend, and her brother, Jack, the spitting image of their dad, was as excited as she was about the idea of learning to sail, and the two of them waited impatiently for Robert to turn up. Jack's dark hair was standing up in spikes the way it always did when he ran his hands through it distractedly as he talked, his eyes fixed on the road outside.

'Do you think we can drop the anchor and have a picnic?' he mused.

'I expect so,' agreed Elsie, closing her eyes dreamily for a moment to imagine the feeling of the boat rocking beneath her.

The day looked promising. There was warmth to the sun already, and the leaves of the silver birch by the gate shivered gently in the breeze. Elsie smiled to herself and opened her eyes just in time to see her uncle pulling into the drive in his old, battered car., swinging wide to allow clearance for the trailer hitched to the back.

A tiny trailer and a tiny boat. A boat made for two. Elsie and Jack looked at each other in dismay.

'It's titchy,' said Jack, and Elsie felt her heart sink.

She had pictured the day so vividly in her mind's eye, the boat creaming across the harbour with sails and flags flying, all of them together, having a proper family day. Just like they used to before… when they were still a real family.

She squeezed her eyes tightly shut again for a moment, willing the image of her mother to fade so that the sunshine of a moment ago could stay with her a little while longer. She opened them quickly, determinedly banishing the dark and fleeting thought to the back of her mind, and ran downstairs with Jack to greet Robert.

Her fears were realised almost immediately.

'All of us?' Robert said in consternation. 'No, love, I'm sorry, the boat's new to me and I'm only just starting to get to grips with it myself. It's only little and it really can't hold more than two of us at a time. Tell you what, I'll take Jack out first, then if there's time, I'll take you afterwards. There's plenty of tide still to sail with.'

Elsie fled upstairs, biting her lip to hide her disappointment. She watched as her brother helped her uncle push the little boat off the trailer at the end of the slipway from the window in her tiny bedroom. Out, straight into the now stiff breeze and jauntily heeling over as she picked up speed, leaving Elsie behind with the certainty of a local girl that this was not the high tide Robert thought it was, this was the second of the unusual 'double high,' something only seen in shallow harbours like Christchurch, with a narrow, fast neck to the open sea, the infamous 'Run' at Mudeford.

The tide would soon be dropping, leaving Uncle Robert and Jack with a slow, hard slog back to the slipway. Although this gave Elsie a certain sly satisfaction, it did little to wash away the bitter taste of the child left out and left behind.

Robert left the next day, knowing that he had upset her, but not knowing how to make her feel better. He hugged her and said goodbye, his gruffness belying his anxiety, but her father rounded on her as soon as he had gone and told her to 'wipe that miserable look off her face and get on with cooking breakfast.'

She escaped shortly after they had eaten, breakfast taken over the kitchen table with the three of them stunned into a silence borne of tension, guilt, and resentment. Later, down at the beach, she found a sharp stick and stabbed the cold, unfeeling sand until her fingers ached. And when she got home to the little cottage that night, she went upstairs and dragged her wooden bed across the landing into the tiny box room that was still crammed with all her mother's clothes, and neither Jack nor Dad dared to meet her stony gaze when she came down to make her cocoa to take to her new abode.

The summer passed, and Jack went back to school. He gave her an awkward hug as the porter lifted his trunk onto the train from the platform, aware that a balance had shifted during this holiday, that the easy relationship they had always enjoyed had been tested and found wanting.

Elsie wanted, more than anything else, to give him her usual heartfelt squeeze but found that she couldn't do this. She was still angry that he hadn't stuck up for her to sail, but in the same instant, knowing that it was not his fault, it was simply a question of time and tide, not to mention the elder brother's divine right to go first. She gazed at him, speechless with lost opportunity as he loaded his trunk onto the obliging trolley of the long-suffering porter, hope fluttering in her chest that he would turn to make a move towards her, make some gesture to say sorry for their wash out of a summer, a gesture to make it right.

Jack did nothing. Nothing but an awkward wave, his eyes and mind turning to the easy friendship he enjoyed with his school friends, the camaraderie of the school train embracing and concealing him from her along with the choking smoke.

As his train chugged slowly off into the distance, she turned on her heel and walked sombrely back home alone, home to Dad and his moods and his uncomprehending anger that Mum had just walked out, just like that, leaving him with an insatiable need for sustenance that nobody, nobody else could provide. She found it hard to deal with his need for food, vast meals three times a day, every day. Sometimes she found it hard to believe that it could already be time to start cooking again, after all, hadn't she just finished cleaning up after the last meal?

The lost, biddable eleven-year-old she'd been then did not sit well with the rebellious fourteen-year-old she was becoming. Her grief when Mum left had been met with hugs and mutual tears then – now, her dad rarely threw her a kind look, and she'd become chained to the kitchen in a way that she now resented, missing her freedom, missing Jack, and most of all, missing Mum.

Elsie was the last to understand that her father could not bear to look at her. That, as she grew up, he could not bear to see her hazel eyes and the pain they held, nor to hold her young frame that reminded him so starkly of the woman that had walked away from their lives and left them all.

BEYOND TIDE AND TIME

Chapter 2

Three Years Previously: 1933

Elsie awoke suddenly, conscious only of the warmth of her blankets and the sound of her heart beating hard in her chest.

Something had woken her, but she wasn't sure what. She lay very still, breathing as quietly as she could manage, and gradually her ears attuned to the murmur of voices in the kitchen below. The voices rose and fell, and she lay listening without curiosity and beginning to drowse again when the sound of a chair being scraped back so hard it must have fallen snatched her back out of sleep once more.

She sat up and looked over at Jack's bed, her eyes finding the whites of his in the gloom.

'What's going on?' he whispered, but she shook her head and motioned towards the door. Jack wriggled out of his blankets just as she did, both wincing as their bare feet touched the cold wooden floorboards.

They crept out of the door without a word and crouched on the landing, anxious to hear what was being said in the kitchen below. The eleven-year-old girl and her brother, her closest friend and companion at three years her senior, huddled together in complicit silence as they strained to hear something they wished later they had never witnessed, their bare toes curling up against the cold. At first, they heard their dad shouting, but then, to their surprise, the furious voice of their mother had risen over this, and now all they could hear was low, unintelligible muttering with occasional louder exclamations.

Suddenly, they heard a noise they had rarely heard before in their young lives, and Elsie raised horrified eyes to meet Jack's as they both realised it was the sound of their mother sobbing. Again, Dad's voice rose, but this time, the angry retort from Mum was cut short by the harsh sound of a slap, the abrupt noise reverberating in the sudden, echoing silence. The kitchen door opened then, and the children froze, their mother's voice reaching them with icy clarity from the hallway directly beneath their feet.

'You're right, Bill,' said Mum bitterly, 'I don't understand. How can I, when you won't tell me what happened to you? All I know is what I read in the papers after Jutland. I know it was a sea battle, and I also know it was bloody years ago.. Beyond that, I have no idea what happened to my own husband. Maybe I'm supposed to know why you won't take the kids sailing, why you drink like this, but I don't have a bloody crystal ball. And I will not be hit by you again, I will not.'

And with that, she carefully and deliberately unhooked her best coat from the hooks in the hallway and walked out of the front door without a backwards glance at the two children at the top of the stairs.

Then silence. Elsie turned huge, terrified eyes to Jack, and as the role of big brother settled heavily on his shoulders, he took her icy hands and led her back to their bedroom. And much later, when he became aware of her standing lost and bereft by his bed, he flicked back the covers wordlessly and the two children clung to each other in the wreckage of the sleepless night that followed.

***

Elsie woke the next morning, surprised to find that that the sun was already pouring into their room, and she could hear sounds in the kitchen below. She sat up and swung her legs round, realising as she felt the empty dent in the bed next to her that Jack must already be up.

She went downstairs, her bare feet pattering on the wooden boards as she went into the sunny little kitchen. There, hell appeared to have broken loose, and she paused, staring around her as she took in what was happening.

Jack was kneeling by the stove, his face covered in soot as he poked ineffectually at the stubbornly unlit coals. There was a dirty plate and mug on the table, but there was no sign of Dad, Mum, or their breakfast.

'Morning,' she said uncertainly, and Jack jumped at the sound of her voice.

'It won't light,' he said unnecessarily, and to her horror, he burst into tears, wiping the back of his hand across his face and smearing tears and soot as he did so.

Elsie was so taken aback by his outburst that she stood, dumbfounded, then steadily began what would be her task for years to come, unwanted but hers, nevertheless.

She sent the snivelling Jack out to get the milk from the front step and knelt in front of the stove, blowing and coaxing patiently until a hot little jet of flame took hold. Then she stood and put the kettle on, soothed by the hiss and then the reassuring whistle as she made tea for them both.

And later, when Jack returned with his face washed and ready for breakfast, neither of them mentioned their mother, and when, or indeed if, she might be coming home.

The days fell into a sort of pattern that summer. They would get up as soon as they heard Dad moving about, and Elsie would light the stove and get breakfast on. Sleep in her eyes, she soon learnt to cook him an egg or something substantial after the first time he shouted at her for just providing fresh bread and butter. As soon as he left to go to work at the shop, she and Jack would breathe a sigh of relief and Jack would swing out the door to meet up with his friends as soon as he could. Elsie would begin clearing up the breakfast things and start planning lunch, knowing that Dad would be home at 12.30 and expecting it to be on the table.

Elsie did not question this new order. Jack was her big brother and had always done whatever Jack wanted, and she was too afraid of her dad's new brooding demeanour to argue her case with him.

And now, three years older and much angrier, as this summer waned, so did that most precious bond with her once beloved sibling, such that when the train chugged away along the cold, hard tracks, her mind had already turned away and her heart had hardened. From this point on, Elsie needed to learn to survive with her father.

Alone.

CHAPTER 3

Daniel: 1936

A few days after Jack left for school, Elsie returned to her own school in Mudeford.

It was actually a relief, she reflected, as she sat contemplating the blackboard full of sums which would previously have struck dread into her heart – now they just seemed insubstantial and irrelevant compared to the daily struggle of life at home. Life which had worsened that morning as she had to light the fire early to heat the iron to press her uniform, and by the time she'd done this, paying meticulous attention to the sleeves as Mum always had, the fire burnt too low for her to stoke it up in time to cook her dad's usual enormous breakfast. He had yelled at her loud enough for her to almost wet herself, but after he slammed out of the door, she crammed her rather damp drawers into the bottom of the laundry basket, slipped on her neatly pressed blouse and left with her head held high.

It felt peaceful at school. The drone of the teacher's voice soothed her agitated mind, and gradually the morning's anger slipped away as she watched a bumble bee batter itself clumsily against the window, again and again as it reached for the sunlight streaming in.

She awoke abruptly, the dust still swirling wildly in the air where the teacher must have thrown the board rubber at her. She jerked upright, mortified as she became aware of the hushed giggles around her, the other girls talking behind their hands and Miss Jupp, a teacher she'd always loved and admired, standing over her with fury in her eyes. Elsie took one look, and for the second time that day, her courage failed her.

She pushed back her chair, leapt to her feet, and blind to the startled look in the eyes of her favourite teacher, she fled. Fled out of the hot classroom, down the corridor with her school shoes clattering on the boards, out of the little yard with the hopscotch painstakingly marked out for generations of skilful feet, and across the road to the edge of the harbour.

Off came her shoes, down came her hair, and Elsie was free to run into the sea, her toes clenching to find some grip in the mud, her skin tingling with the stinging cold of the water, her beautifully pressed blouse hanging out of her skirt, splashed now with water and spattered with silt. Panting with rage and release, her eyes stinging with salt and the breeze across the sea, she stopped at last, allowing her breathing to calm along with the ripples playing against her legs.

'You all right?'

Elsie jumped at the sound of the voice, shielded her eyes with her hands against the glare of the sun on the water. A few yards away, she saw the silhouette of a boat, then as its partially raised mainsail flapped across the sun and shielded her eyes, a vision swam hazily into focus.

A wooden boat, a fishing boat with crab pots and lines strewn on the deck. A dark red sail hanging loosely from the mast, flapping gently in the failing breeze. A young man dressed in torn shorts and a fisherman's smock was squinting at her curiously, concern etched upon his young face as he stared at her, standing thigh deep in the muddy water, her skirt floating unheeded about her.

'You all right?' he asked again, uncertainly, the worry on his face apparent to Elsie as she peered up at him.

'Can I get on?' she asked impulsively and was rewarded with a beaming smile.

'I'm Daniel,' he said as he stretched out a hand to help her up. She caught it, momentarily surprised at the firmness of his grip, and swung up out of the cold water and onto the wooden deck.

Daniel sat down on one of the upturned crab pots, and the two sat, each silently taking stock of the other.

Daniel saw a young girl, hands chapped and reddened beyond her years, tear stains on her cheeks. But what struck him was her hair, curly tresses falling over her face, a tanned and lightly freckled face with hazel eyes, red-rimmed now with crying but almond-shaped and framed by dark lashes.

Elsie saw a tall lad, around the same age as Jack, but broader and sturdier in build, confidence radiating from his blue eyes as he smiled at her encouragingly. Blond shaggy hair, faded clothes, and bare feet, he could have been a sailor from just about any period of time from Nelson to the present day. As she glanced around, her nose twitched at the strong smell of fish, but she saw that the deck itself was scrupulously scrubbed and clean. Lines were neatly coiled, and the deck was clear except for the pile of crab and lobster pots stacked carefully to one side.

All of a sudden, Daniel's face cracked into a wide smile, then he started to laugh.

'What is it?' snapped Elsie, stung by his easy humour, then began to smile herself as his infectious chuckles continued unchecked.

'I suppose you must be all right, even though you still haven't actually said anything yet,' he spluttered, and Elsie grinned apologetically.

'School, you know,' she mumbled. 'I've just had enough. So I walked out and here I am.' She raised her eyes then, and for the first time, she smiled directly at Daniel, cheekily challenging him to remonstrate with her.

'I haven't been to school for ages,' he answered, suddenly looking grim. 'I took over the boat from my dad. Been fishing ever since, not really had time for schoolwork, too.' He turned away abruptly, and Elsie felt the chill as if a cloud had covered the sun.

'Sorry,' she said, feeling that she must have upset him but not really understanding why.

He half-turned back towards her and threw her a wry look.

'Anyhow, on a day like this, who needs school?' He grinned conspiratorially. 'Fancy coming fishing?'

CHAPTER 4

Fishing for Freedom

Hours later, Elsie crept up the slipway in her bare feet, her school shoes held up high out of the water and her eyes scanning to see if anyone had seen her return. She had no clear idea exactly what time it was, but she was fairly sure that Dad wouldn't be home yet, so would be none the wiser about her walking out of school. She was fourteen now anyway, she reasoned, so the school wouldn't have sent a note to tell him that she'd walked out.

She ran the short way along the bank back to the old row of cottages, all fishermen's cottages in the past, but since the Great War, so few men had returned in a fit state to carry on that now less than a quarter of them were still owned by any local salties. Her dad used to be a fisherman, but that was years ago, way before she and Jack had been born. He had returned from the war injured, so she'd been told, although she was unsure what this injury was, precisely, and Jack had been hazy when she'd pressed him for details. She suspected he didn't know either. He looked all right to her, apart from his temper. He had worked in the shop for as long as she could remember, and as far as she knew, hadn't picked up a rod or reel in her lifetime.

She let herself in the back door, warily peering through the window first. The kitchen was empty, and she breathed a sigh of relief as she knelt before the range to light the fire, long burnt out.

The creak of the door alerted her to his presence, and she whirled around as he walked through, his face dark as thunder.

'I'm sorry, Dad,' she faltered, gazing up at him as her courage failed her. Tears prickling her eyelids for the third time that day, she backed away, holding up her hands to ward away the slap she was sure she had coming.

'Where the hell is my dinner?' he thundered.

Elsie stuttered in fright. 'I'm just doing it now, Dad. I was shopping for more eggs,' she improvised, knowing that he wouldn't have looked in the pantry, what he considered as her domain, after all, to check up on her.

'You're late. You know I come back hungry. I've done a day's work before you even get to school. Now get a move on.'

He snatched his newspaper off the kitchen table and turned on his heel. Elsie listened, scarcely daring to breathe until she heard the creak of the rocker in the front room, and collapsed as her legs gave way, trembling into one of the wooden kitchen chairs.

He didn't know about school, of that she was pretty certain. She just had to rustle up an omelette as fast as she could and he'd leave her be, so she turned to the stove again, relieved to see the flames flaring and heartily glad that she'd stocked up in the market last week and had plenty of eggs. Her tracks were covered for now.

***

The next day dawned bright and breezy, the wind knocking the white caps off the choppy waves out near the Run.

Elsie had slept heavily and dreamt deeply, succumbing to the sleepiness instilled by the day's sea air the moment she climbed under her blankets. She woke with Daniel in her mind. She could see him clearly, the sun shining through his scruffy blond thatch, and she smiled to herself.

Quickly, she jumped out of bed, and curling her toes against the morning chill, she scurried downstairs to get the stove fired up and her dad's breakfast on as fast as she could.

'Bacon?' he asked in surprise, sniffing the air appreciatively as he followed her into the kitchen a few minutes later, his unshaven face grazing her cheek as he dropped his usual perfunctory kiss. She tried not to wince away – last night's beer stale on his breath – and gave him her brightest smile.

'I'm sorry I got a bit behind last night, Dad,' she said. 'I just wanted to give you a bit of a treat today to say sorry.'

She looked up at him slyly through her lashes, and to her relief, he grinned at her.

'I do like a bacon sandwich to start my day. Stock taking today too, so I shan't be home for lunch, and I'll probably be a bit late tonight too. I'll get some fish and chips for us both. It's been a while since we had a fish supper and I'll be famished by the time I get in.'

Elsie smiled and turned to hide her guilt as she wrapped him up some bread and jam to take with him for a bite at lunchtime. As soon as he told her he'd be late, all thoughts of returning to school had vanished.

She was going to meet Daniel.

***

He was waiting for her, just as she'd hoped. The boat's deck was wet as if he'd just washed it down, and as she waded out to his swinging mooring, he turned quickly, as if he had been hoping but not quite believing she would come.

'Hello,' she said shyly.

Then all traces of awkwardness evaporated as he replied, 'Hop aboard then.' his face fairly cracking with a huge smile.

She liked it that he didn't ask questions. That he told her how to untie the line for the scuffed old buoy, showed her how to coil it properly without it twisting. That when they were through the Run with his arms pulling hard on the long, scuffed wooden oars to get them through the channel, he took her hands and put them on the tiller, explaining how she was going to turn the boat into the wind while he put the sail up. He didn't laugh at her when she shrieked as the boat heeled over at first, showed her how to hold her course. And as each day rolled into the next, she became more and more confident, and came to love the way Daniel trusted her to do more and more tasks without waiting for instruction.

The week came to an end, and with it, so did the prospect of sailing again with her newfound companion. Elsie could see no way of getting out while her dad was around at the weekend, and worse still, the tides were so late for the coming week that she wouldn't be able to go out and get back in time. The time yawned ahead of her emptily with no respite in sight, and she was very quiet as she helped tie the boat up that last, perfect afternoon.

'Don't worry about it,' said Daniel, sensing her distress. 'The tide'll come good again. You know where I am, and you should spend time with your dad when he's not at work, anyway.'

She scowled at him fiercely when he said that, and he glowered back in return.

'You really should,' he insisted.

'What do you know about it, anyway?' snapped Elsie, hating his assumption that all was well in their little home. 'I'm just the unpaid help. He wouldn't notice if it was me or some other skivvie so long as the food gets stuck in front of him.' She turned away, breathless and irritated, then suddenly realised that Daniel hadn't answered. She turned her face towards his silence, and saw, to her chagrin, that his head was in his hands.

'What have I said?' she asked horrified, and when he shook his head in answer, she knelt in front of him and took his hands gently away from his face, saw the tears rolling down his sunburnt cheeks as his mouth worked while he fought for control. 'Tell me, Daniel, I won't tell a soul.'

He blinked hard and met her eye, and a watery smile broke through at the sight of her on her knees among the buckets full of crabs.

'My dad's dead,' he answered brusquely, and Elsie squeezed his hands tightly and stayed silent, waiting for more. 'He got gassed in the war. He used to cough and cough…' He broke off, the tears pouring down his face again, and with a huge effort, he wiped them with the back of a hand and carried on. 'He went back to fishing afterwards, but he kept catching a chill. He made it through until last winter. You remember how cold it was here?' Elsie nodded, remembering, but said nothing, unwilling to interrupt. 'He got a cold and then it went on his chest.' He took a deep, shuddering breath. 'Then he just upped and died. Just like that. They said it was pneumonia. Mum died when she had me, so I never knew her anyway, but I miss Dad so much.'

He broke off and Elsie put her arms round him then, silently clinging to each other for companionship and comfort.

'My dad isn't like he used to be,' Elsie confided. 'Mum left us. They had a fight, and I don't know where she went. She never wrote…' She broke off, her voice faltering, and Daniel returned her hug. 'He used to fish too, years ago before the war, but he gave it up. I think he's given everything up, actually.' She finished in a rush of words, and Daniel pulled away to look at her, his face creased with concern.

'I still think he needs you,' he ventured, and Elsie nodded, stiffly.

'I'll try.'

***

The next fortnight seemed an eternity to Elsie. She went back to school, ignoring the questioning looks from her teachers, kept her head down and worked hard. She shopped and cooked diligently, ensuring that Dad was kept happy and full of the best food she could muster. She shopped carefully too, getting supplies that would keep well and could be cooked up into a decent meal in a short time. Guiltily remembering Daniel's words, she also did her best to be nice to him, but honestly, she thought sadly, maybe it was too late for that? Each night he ate his dinner, pushed his chair back and buried his head in his newspaper, cutting short all efforts on her part at conversation, until she was left, staring mutely at the back of his paper until she gave up and went to bed. Come Friday and Saturday nights, he was off down the Mudeford Working Men's Club anyway, so she barely saw him at all.

She actually rather enjoyed the evenings to herself when he'd gone for his pint. The little cottage was cosy enough when she lit the fire each evening, her but her attention was always elsewhere, her eyes out on the harbour, surreptitiously watching for Daniel to return. Each night, the tide was later and later, but each time she saw his little boat with the jaunty light hanging from the mast pulling its way up to its mooring, the oars creaking quietly in the rowlocks, she breathed a sigh of relief that he was back safely.

And the day that she knew the tides were in her favour again, she was ready and waiting.

***

Daniel grinned at her as he pulled hard on the oars, and she squinted at him against the bright light of the early sun on the water.

'You all right?' he asked and they both burst out laughing as they recognised what had become their own little catch phrase.

'I'm all right,' Elsie replied, and as she leant back against the gunwale, she realised that she was actually happier than she had been for a long time.

Daniel had stepped into the shoes that Jack appeared to have vacated without a backwards glance. She missed her brother more than she could admit, but his letters were short and infrequent, smacking of duty rather than a wish to stay connected. She sighed, remembering that day when he'd gone out with Robert – that had been the start of it, she pondered wistfully. They had been so close before, just the two of them sticking up for each other in the face of Dad's moods. Never talking about Mum but understanding when the other had a 'down' day, each knowing when a hug was needed, or space to be alone to miss her and wish that things were different. Since that day, his withdrawal had been steady but absolute; he seemed unwilling or unable to connect with her in any other than the superficial way that she'd become accustomed to from their father. It was only now, in the companionship of her new friend, that Elsie truly recognised the depth of her loneliness, a child abandoned by her mother and cast adrift by her father and most treasured brother, alone but not yet old enough or free to find another path.

With Daniel, she was able to talk. To tell him about the night Mum left, the betrayal she felt that her own mother had left her behind, walked away from her own flesh and blood without a backwards glance. Tears running freely as the wind blew through her hair sailing out over Christchurch Ledge. Holding the tiller steady as Daniel baited and dropped the crab pots one by one, the plaited willow reeds creaking in protest as he heaved them over the side. Turning the boat back to the Run as the tide began to turn, making the return journey possible for the little boat and its tired rower. She talked and talked and talked, grateful that he never interrupted. He simply listened and understood, the light from the water reflecting on his face as he regarded her, wishing he could help. He didn't realise just how much he already was helping the lonely girl, abandoned by her mother, misunderstood by her brother, and avoided by her father.

'Catch,' he said suddenly, and Elsie squealed in alarm as he threw something towards her across the pile of crab pots between them. She threw him a look of disgust as the cold, glistening fish slithered through her hands onto the sun-warmed deck.

'What was that for?' she demanded, retrieving the smelly mackerel with some difficulty, hurling it into a bucket and curling her lip in disgust as she wiped her hands on the front of her dad's old smock, which she'd long ago appropriated for fishing trips with Daniel.

'Fishing, stupid.' He laughed but wiped the grin hurriedly off his face when Elsie shot him a glare. 'All right, all right,' he conceded. 'Different fishing. As soon as we've dropped the last of the pots, we're going to try to catch us some serious fish. Fancy a bit of bass for your tea?'

Elsie smiled, and Daniel caught his breath as her face lit up with some memory surfacing from the depths.

'Mum loved it when Dad used to buy fish from Mudeford,' she said, clinging on hard to the feeling that had taken hold so suddenly, an all-encompassing feeling of home, of family and of love. Tears started in her eyes just as fast as it faded, and as Daniel saw the light dim, he reached across to give her a hard hug as she burst into tears.

'I'm sorry,' she muttered. 'I didn't mean to spoil it. I just miss her... in little waves that come at me from nowhere.'

'It's always there, though, isn't it,' he replied, and Elsie nodded through her tears. 'It's always there, just in the background, then suddenly it comes to the surface and I'm just never ready for it.'

Daniel squeezed her tight, then released her abruptly.

'Time to get on with it,' he chided gently. 'I want you to learn to fish properly and I'm not getting caught by the tide for you or all the tea in China.'

***

Elsie went home that night with sunburnt cheeks, a heart full of love for her new friend, and a beautiful sea bass for their tea. She slipped out of her smock in the bottom of the garden and stuffed it away in a bag she kept hidden in the little shed where the remains of her dad's old fishing gear leant, rotting sadly against the wall.

She wrapped the fish carefully in newspaper, then skipped jauntily to the kitchen door to get on with tea before Dad got in, the warmth and happiness of the day still lingering with her as she turned the latch.

And then her eyes took in the scene before her, her breath stopping in her throat and a chill hitting her as if the temperature had suddenly plummeted.

Miss Jupp, her favourite teacher, eyes looking at her searchingly as they took in the sunburn, the hastily wiped hands, the parcel of fresh fish. But much worse, her dad's face, disappointment and fury vying for position as he stared at his errant daughter.

Chapter 5

Under Lock and Key: 1938

The next few days were purgatory.

Miss Jupp had told Dad about her perfunctory attendance that term, there for a week, then gone again with no word of explanation. She pointed out again and again that Elsie was free to leave as she pleased. She was past the legal age now, but that this toing and froing was disastrous for a girl showing promise. Elsie was bright, she insisted, and could become a very adept secretary or even consider a career in a respectable profession such as nursing, should she care to put her mind to it.

Throughout, Elsie was aware of the cold fury emanating from her father and was rewarded by a hard slap across her face the moment that Miss Jupp had left, casting a concerned look at her brightest pupil even as the door closed firmly in her face.

'Dad,' she protested, but he was incandescent with rage and would hear no plea for mercy.

Bit by bit, he wore her down until the whole story was laid bare before him. The truancy, the subterfuge, the betrayal. His own daughter, going out to sea without his knowledge or consent, the jealousy of her freedom and his frustration at his own inability to go back to the life he had loved sliding a cold blade of injustice deep into his heart.

There would be no more fishing.

Elsie was going back to school.

***

1938

Elsie waded out late one night when the moon was bright and the harbour still and silent, the only ripples made by her bare legs as she waded towards the wooden boat creaking peaceably on its mooring.

Many months had gone by. Days of yearning for the sea, bitter nights of missing Daniel.

Months, much to her surprise, of discovering pleasure in learning again, the lessons gently reminding her that there was a world to be discovered as yet unknown and unmet, a world that her teachers wanted her to share.

But finally, she awoke one night, knowing that she had to make contact, that she had to get some kind of message to him to explain her abrupt absence.

She wrote to him during her last lesson at school the next day. Her friends' heads were bent over their appointed essays, her own finished as quickly as she was able. Time bought, a safe, private moment.

The words wouldn't come. She twisted the pencil anxiously in her hand, painfully aware of the clock ticking inexorably onwards towards the end of the school day.

'I'm sorry.' She wrote, horrified by her hasty scrawl when she'd meant to write something meaningful, something poignant to her treasured friend. 'It's Dad. He found out and I can't come again. I'm so sorry.'

Before she slipped out that night, she unfolded the little scrap of paper, hoping to find some other words, but realising that there were none.

She gripped the slippery mud with her bare toes, feeling the sharpness of shells underfoot. Reaching out an icy hand, she hauled herself up over the transom, scraping her legs painfully on the wooden edge as she scrambled aboard. She sat for a long moment, intensely aware of the rough wood under her wet feet, the smell of the crab pots and the quiet creak and sway of the boom. Tears welling again, she stood and jammed the little note under a cleat, knowing he would spot it as soon as he released the main sheet to sail. She took one last deep breath, savouring the sounds and smells that she'd come to love so much, then slid without a backward glance over the side.

***

God, he missed her. Each day, the same routine, each day an hour later with the tide, glancing across to the row of fishermen's cottages, hoping but not really believing that he might see her, standing with shoes in her hand, waiting to be invited aboard.

Daniel was lonely, so lonely that some days he talked to himself just to hear a voice out loud.

Lonely and afraid. Daniel was the first to admit that he was not a good fisherman. He had been too young to learn the ropes from his father, precious gems handed down from generation to generation, father to son. By the time he was old enough, his dad was too sick, and now it was too late.

He hung around the town quay a lot, watching the other men working in the shadow of the old Priory. Learning how to coil his lines properly, how to mend his crab pots and re-weave any broken strands of willow before they came adrift. Most of the men knew his story and would have helped if he had had the courage to ask, but since the war, many of them were struggling with their own problems and fighting their own demons and were not ready to take on a hungry apprentice. Somehow his very sense of isolation served to keep him apart, each day he walked past the men loading their pots and tackle for the day and, out of respect for his dead father, they would fall silent, unwittingly making him more self-conscious and even more alone.

Wading out to his boat, his heart ached. Casting a glance across to the fishermen's cottages on the bank, their facades shuttered and closed against him, he sighed deeply. There would be no Elsie for company today.

He slipped his lines as quickly as he could and bent his back to the oars, as yet unaware of the note fluttering in the cleat.

***

Elsie fell into a habit of watchfulness, and she knew he had gone as soon as she got back from school, her first glance from the kitchen window confirming the empty mooring in the creek.

She checked morning and night, jealous when she saw him gone, reassured when she saw that he was back safely. Sometimes the tides were so late that she would watch from her bedroom window, eyes scanning the harbour for the little white lantern he always slung from the bow when night fell.

Today, of all days, she thought of him, and the intensity of her memory shocked her, the clarity with which she could see his dirty blond hair ruffled in the wind, his bare feet on the deck, his broad smile and the hard muscles of his back as he bent to haul in the pots. Thought of him and missed him so acutely that her breath caught in her chest, the pain making her double over as she leant against the window-ledge.

The tide would be late tonight, she realised. She wouldn't be able to spot him as he came in, but she would look for his light, she vowed to herself. She turned away abruptly to focus on the task in hand – cooking, as ever, to placate her increasingly taciturn father, and did her best to put Daniel out of her mind.

Hours later, she awoke abruptly, and lay listening quietly to discover what noise, what tiny shift in the wind outside might have awakened her from her slumber. But then she knew, without needing to check, that the boat was not safely back on its mooring.

Daniel had not returned with the tide.

Elsie stood at her window with her heart pounding wildly, her eyes sweeping the channel for any flicker of light, which might be-lie the truth which she already instinctively knew.

She knew that she would see nothing. She knew Daniel needed help, that something had befallen the young, lone fisherman, and that she was the only one who could guess at his plight.

And with all the courage that she could muster, she knocked firmly on her father's door and walked in to wake him and throw herself, and Daniel, upon his mercy.

Chapter 6

Rescue and Redemption

B ill rose to the challenge. Humbled and proud, Elsie watched him take charge, putting behind him the years of avoidance, the years of denial of his boundless love and paralysing fear of the sea.

They ran to the town quay together, panting hard as they swung aboard a fishing boat that Elsie recognised. It belonged to a fisherman who always nodded as she and Daniel rowed past, a man it seemed that Dad knew but no longer talked to.

As she looked at him, questions in her eyes, he grunted,

'It's Martin's boat. He would understand.'

As he reached for the oars, Elsie slipped the lines and felt the boat surge out into the tide, her prow finding the current of the run, now running out to sea at the end of the first high tide, the tide that should have seen Daniel safely home. As the boat lifted to the pull of the oars, the wooden blades cleaving through the water, she looked in awe at the expression on her father's face. His eyes were shut, his shoulders were bulging with the strain.

And he was smiling.

Smiling at the feel of the spray, smiling at the smell of the salt and the bleached wooden boards and the empty crab pots. Tears starting in his eyes at the joy of the surging current as he pulled for Daniel's life but feeling as if he were pulling for his own.

They found him as the moon rose high above Hengistbury Head, the silver light catching on the silhouette of the little boat lolling at the mercy of the waves. Elsie scrambling over the gunwales to climb aboard the stricken vessel, her boom swinging uselessly in the night breeze, her skipper unconscious on the deck below. His shattered leg sticking out at an angle beneath his crumpled body, blood congealing stickily on the boards beneath his ashen face.

Elsie would never forget the night her father came back. Became again the man her mother had once loved… a man of the sea with decision and independence and fortitude on his brow. Shaking her head in wordless gratitude as he helped her bandage Daniel's bruised and bleeding head, splinting his leg as best as they could with the wooden tiller from his boat as they tied it up to their own and began the long pull back to await the turn of the tide, riding the second high of the night up the Run and back into the safety of the harbour, tying up alongside the quay just as it began to come alive with the fishermen and traders coming to buy the nights takings, the fish stall sending a runner to get help when they took in the scene before their eyes, Elsie kneeling with Daniel's head resting on her thighs and her hands steadying him, feeling the rise and fall of his chest as he hissed against the pain, now conscious but barely able to speak through his clenched teeth.

And her father's arms catching her and carrying her home when the ambulance took Daniel and her legs finally let her down and gave way beneath her.

* * *

The next few days passed in a blur of tears, hospital visits, and endless, priceless talking.

The shortest to hear, but nonetheless hard to bear, was Daniel's story.

He had found her note as he let the mainsheet free, and had spent the day desolate, catching very little and sick at heart with loneliness. He had decided to call it a day and leave as soon as the tide made the return trip possible, but as he went to drop the sail, a squall had caught the little boat and the boom had twitched viciously, catching his head with a glancing blow that sent him sprawling across the deck, his leg twisting beneath him as he went down.

The head wound was superficial. Head wounds always bleed a lot, the doctor assured them, but the fractured leg was more serious. It needed surgery to help knit the bones together, and Daniel could expect to be bedridden and in traction for some weeks to come.

The day after his operation, Elsie went to visit him, forcing herself not to allow pity to show on her face as she looked down at the dressings hiding his poor, twisted leg.

'You all right?' she asked and was rewarded with a ghost of a smile on his ashen face as he heard his own words on her lips. She held his hand and shushed him as he tried to find the words to thank her for coming to find him that dark night.

'I always looked for you,' she confessed, 'and I knew something must have happened to you, or to the boat. But Dad was incredible, Daniel. I don't think I could have just taken a boat and come to you like that on my own.'

Daniel squeezed her hand, his eyes filling with exhausted tears.

'I've missed you,' he said simply. 'And I'm so glad to know you were watching out for me. I wish I'd known. I always watched for you too.' He fell silent, the two of them sitting quietly, but their hearts swelling with the depth of their friendship that had come to mean the world to them both.

Over the next few weeks, Daniel grew stronger, but he was not the strong, hardy lad she'd known. His leg healed, but not well. Weeks of traction, weeks of suffering, but worse was to come when the splints came off. His face turning bitter and dark as the doctors told him, in gentle tones to deliver the harshest of news, that he would need crutches for the rest of his life. That the shattered bone of his femur would never unite well enough to take his weight unaided. That he would never be able to fish for a living, and that it was time to sell the boat and look for a desk job.

Daniel turned his face away from them and refused to discuss it any further.

***

It took much longer to hear Dad's story, both of them needing to stop frequently to search for the courage to carry on talking and listening. After many years of silence, Elsie and he finally found the courage to talk about what they had loved and lost. They talked about Elsie's mum, Betsy, Dad's eyes rising to meet hers in shock when she confessed that she and Jack had heard some of what was said that night, and although Elsie didn't admit to it, the guilt on his face told her that he realised they must have heard him slap her.

His story emerged, haltingly. His voice cracking and breaking in the shuttered darkness of their kitchen, as he described his terrible fear of the sea since the night his ship went down at Jutland. Being plucked from the sea by another ship, the relief of rescue being shattered minutes later by the sight of the nearby *HMS Indefatigable* being hit.

Only two survived that, he told her, so many good men, so many souls lost.

He did try, he said. They had married very young and had only a few short weeks together before he left to fight. When he returned four long years later, Betsy, the soon to be mother of his children and the love of his life, was a wild and carefree spirit, she wanted to spread her wings and enjoy life after the fears and deprivations of war, she wanted freedom, excitement, and joy.

He did try to go back to the sea when he returned from the Navy, and although he found he could manage in the daytime, the dark, implacable surface of the waves at night rendered him incapable of thought and deed. He sold the boat that had been passed to him by his father and from his grandfather in turn, years of tradition, blood, and toil, and turned his face from the sea. He died a little death that day and Betsy marked the change in him, seeing the strong sailor she'd once loved slowly shrinking into a dry, bitter man. Their marriage began to wither with each day that he stayed away from the harbour, unable to look at the water without feeling it, and her taunting him.

Then, after she'd gone, he had to learn to look after his children alone, alongside the pain and bitterness that he was not enough for her, and she'd not loved him enough even to stay for the sake of her children.

What kind of mother could just walk away, he asked Elsie, helplessly in the quiet dark of their kitchen, tears soaking into the scrubbed wood of the table, and she was unable to answer the question which had consumed her too since the night her mother had left.

Watching Jack sailing off with Robert without so much as a backwards glance, his heart had broken in grief for what he had been unable to pass on and enjoy with his children. When he had discovered that Elsie was sailing too, he had been hit by such a wave of fear that he had been consumed by it, fear turning to rage as he sought to keep her safe. And sitting in the cocoon of darkness, night after night, their soft voices rising and falling with the emotion of those memories, he finally raised bleak eyes to meet hers, raising them in defence but finding forgiveness in his daughter's gentle expression and comfort in her arms.

Time passed, and as the months slid by, Daniel underwent more surgery, more pain, and more disappointment. It took four operations and as many months for him to realise that the doctors had probably been right.

And eventually, as the soft light of those spring evenings lengthened into summer, with the rift between father and daughter changed into a powerful bond, Daniel was discharged from hospital and Jack came home.

CHAPTER 7

The Path to War: 1939

Elsie barely recognised him. Not just that her brother had grown from lanky boy to the solid figure of a man, but everything he talked about was alien to her, and disjointed from their simple lives gleaned at the edge of the harbour.

He talked of war. War and aggression, of Germany rearing her greedy head once again, seeking to take what she saw fit for spoils of a war long gone and best forgotten. Of a man named Adolf Hitler, who sought to make her great again, at the expense of the hard-won peace which Europe had enjoyed, despite the ravages of the depression which had befallen them all. Blaming it all on everyone around him, including his own countrymen, as he turned his calculating eyes and raging words upon his neighbours.

And then it was more than words, and just as Jack should have returned to the apprenticeship he had enrolled upon after leaving school, Hitler invaded Poland and Great Britain declared war on Germany.

Elsie, Jack, and their father were crouched around the wireless when the news came, the words crackling like grapeshot falling in the silence of the kitchen.

Daniel was with them. He has spent most of the summer with the family, in fact, and after some quiet words from Bill, he had found work helping out down at the quay, catching lines as the exhausted fishermen came in and sometimes crewing for others as he was still able to man the tiller and hold a straight course while the able-bodied did the heavy work of hauling out the pots.

The four of them looked at each other in silence as the wireless hissed and crackled unheeded now that the announcement had ended, its meaning still heavy in the air.

Jack drew a long, shaky breath.

'I will have to sign up, Dad,' he began, and Dad began to shake his head, slightly at first, then wildly.

'I'm twenty now. I won't have any choice.' He cried as he saw his dad's distress, and suddenly they were all falling together, clutching at each other for comfort on this fearful day.

'I'm so afraid for you,' Dad said. 'I just can't believe it's happening again, after all we went through before. And I'm too old now, I can't help and just the thought of you going alone…' His voice broke.

'I won't be wanted,' observed Daniel, sombrely. 'I'm not a lot of use now, am I?' He poked viciously at his twisted leg with one of his crutches, his face consumed with a rare mixture of guilt and relief, and Bill turned to him, gave him a sad smile.

'Be glad, Daniel, be glad. It's not a game.' And with his mouth working suddenly, he reached out to embrace Elsie, and looking over her shoulders, he added quietly, 'I'm relieved for you, son, and I think we might just need you here.'

***

Much later, Jack lay awake, watching the silver light of the moon reflecting from the harbour up onto his ceiling. He couldn't sleep, and actually he had no desire to. He lay perfectly still, acutely conscious of the sounds and smells of his childhood home, the flickering moonlight mesmerising him as he lay soaking up the feeling of security with every pore of his being. But now knowing, with the bitter pain of adulthood, that it was over, that home would no longer keep them all safe. Or keep them together.

Abruptly, he sat up, throwing back the rough woollen blanket, and as his bare feet hit the cold floorboards, he was reminded, with a choking rush of emotion, of the night his mother had walked out on them all. And how he had looked after Elsie as she crept into his bed for comfort, and how she'd stepped uncomplainingly into his mother's shoes the very next day and begun to look after them all.

He crossed the landing in a single stride, tapped gently on Elsie's door and was rewarded with a quiet murmur of acknowledgment.

Without a word, he flicked back the cover and climbed into the end of her bed, his icy feet gratefully connecting with her warm ones. Their eyes found each other's, bright in the moonlight, and she smiled at him, the bravery of this breaking his heart. And as he began to weep, she sat and rubbed his feet with her hands, this little act of kindness anchoring him and giving him strength.

And they talked. Talked late into the night, Elsie tentatively at first, then her voice growing firmer as she told him what their father had told her, about his fear of sailing since being fished out of the water at Jutland, the bodies of his comrades sliding beneath the waves around him as he struggled for breath in that cold, cold sea. How he had found her out, then put his anger and fear aside to help her save Daniel when she thought all was lost. How close they had become since he confessed his anger and his grief that he had lost his connection with their mother, that their love had not been strong enough to carry them through what they had both suffered and lost because of the Great War, their love foundering in misunderstanding, impatience, and regret.

And Jack told her of his fears. That he wouldn't be good enough, that he might not be brave enough. That he was afraid of injury, that he was afraid to die. And in the cold light of morning, they dressed quietly and walked down to the quay together to meet Daniel so that Jack could say the first of his goodbyes.

And scarcely days later, Elsie had to wave off her brother, her childhood soulmate, not onto the little train to take him back to apprenticeship work, secluded and cocooned from the world, but off on a troop train for training and then bound for France.

CHAPTER 8

First Loss: Late 1939

It was hard to believe there was a war on.

The summer might have slipped into autumn, but the days were long and warm. Elsie continued to go to school, but after long hours of discussion and heated debate with her father, he also now allowed her to take the boat out with Daniel. Elsie was strong and increasingly skilful, perfectly capable of hauling out the pots and retrieving them the next day with their angry occupants snapping with futile claws within. It was worth all the hard work when she would turn to catch Daniel's eye as he sat, balanced on the transom with his twisted leg braced hard against the gunwale and his hands resting on the tiller, finding some kind of peace in being useful, at least enough for this. Her skill with the sails increased, as did her confidence with her patient instructor, and she was happier than she could have believed, the wind though her hair and a good day's catch on the deck before her as they turned for home.

No word came from Jack. He had returned briefly after his training, but had left almost immediately for France, the crisp new uniform sitting stiffly on his young shoulders, weighed down now with a new and unwanted responsibility. Just like the last war, boys forced to become men before their time, some out of a sense of duty, some pushed by others, the cream of England's youth rushing to sign up and offer their lives in the name of peace. Daniel's face taut with guilt and frustration as they parted, Jack trying to find the right words to help him but failing in the face of his own demons. Elsie bridging every divide with her natural warmth and affection, the comfort of her arms enfolding Jack even as he went to step from the platform onto the train full of grim faces. Encircling her brother, her friend and her father with as much love as she could find it within herself to share, and each day making herself carry on, studying, fishing, cooking and providing, falling into bed each night dizzy with fatigue.

But one day, everything changed.

Everything became a little simpler, in some ways, but oh so much sadder.

Elsie swung briskly through the kitchen door after school, reaching for her basket so that she could get to the market before it ended. Stopped abruptly when she saw that she wasn't alone, as she'd expected, and that Dad was there already.

Or in fact, had never left at all, had never made it to work that day, but had simply sat down after she'd gone to school this morning, his heart fluttering strangely in his chest. Realising then that the fluttering was an ending and that he wouldn't have a chance to say his goodbyes to the daughter he loved, nor see his son again, nor an end to this war.

Elsie stood and stared at his still form in the rocking chair, not rocking now but anchored by his dead weight. Stood and wept, shaking with grief until Daniel walked in, alerted to her distress by the sight of the kitchen door swinging unheeded in the breeze. Taking his turn now to rescue her, to bring her back to herself from the dark place she'd retreated to as she held tight to her father's lifeless body in the quiet little kitchen by the sea.

***

She wrote to Jack. Bitter tears falling as her pen formed the words she needed to find to help him through the news as his eyes realised what they were reading. Pouring her heart into that sad little missive to help him through as Daniel was helping her now.

And Daniel kept her going each day as she waited and waited. But while word never came from Jack, word did come. It came from her mother. She had been informed about Bill's death, apparently, he had left a letter in his will to be forwarded to her in the event of his demise, and this had found her in her new home in Ramsgate, and she wanted to meet her.

Elsie had no money to get there by train or bus. All she knew was that she suddenly, urgently needed to meet this woman who had left them all, who now professed interest in them as duty befitted. She had no money, she had no idea how long it would take her, but she did have a boat.

Chapter 9

To Ramsgate and Beyond

Daniel stared at her in dismay.

'Oh, Elsie,' he said, shaking his head, 'you just can't. It's so far and you don't know what you're going to find. Just stay here, let her come to you?'

Elsie shook her head, decisively. 'I'm going on my terms, under my own steam,' she said, unequivocally. 'Then I can leave when I want to. I'm not having her walking back into my home and thinking she can just take over.'

Her voice rose shrilly, and Daniel reached out with a steadying hand.

'I understand, I really do,' he said, quietly. 'But if this is what you want, then I'm coming too.' Elsie started to shake her head, but he pressed on. 'We can fish on the way, so we don't spend too much, and it's easier to sail with the two of us.'

Elsie's eyes filled with grateful tears. She had wanted Daniel to come so much, but hadn't dared to ask him, knowing full well how much pain he still suffered from the cruel injury to his leg.

She had spent hours looking at charts she'd found among her dad's possessions and had realised just how tough it would be to sail as far as Ramsgate from Christchurch. Even with the winds in their favour, this would be a long haul.

***

It was worse than she could have imagined.

The first night, they only made it as far as Beaulieu. The wind was against them, meaning a long hard slog, beating up into a capricious easterly wind and getting a soaking as each wave broke against the bow. Rowing up the entrance to the river and anchoring as soon as they could get out of the current, cold and tired, they huddled under the canvas they had packed, stomachs growling with hunger.

They had eaten the sandwiches they had packed, and although they had planned to go ashore to light a fire and cook their freshly caught fish over it, the banks were steep and muddy, and they hadn't the heart to scramble up them in the hope of finding firm, dry land.

They slept fitfully, to be awoken before dawn by a little fleet of fishing boats catching the tide, and within a few moments, they were sitting, stiff with cold with an oar each, pulling out into the current to follow them out to sea.

As soon as they had shipped oars and raised the sails, Elsie busied herself finding them some meagre provisions that they could eat without cooking, milk, a slice of ham and a hunk of cheese each. It was the last of their food, and later that night, she wept with relief as they pulled alongside a quay filled with the familiar sight of baskets of crab and fish and stall holders packing up the market for the day and happy to give their bruised fruit and spoiled vegetables to the two, exhausted sailors.

A safe place to moor and a sheltered hedge to sleep under, the two curled up, back-to-back for warmth, with their bellies full of mackerel and their hearts full of hope.

***

On the third night, the winds were fair, and they sailed steadily, running with the wind, and feeling the miles slip easily beneath the keel as they headed ever eastwards.

The moon was in its infancy and the stars were huge and startling against the navy ink of the night. Elsie had the tiller, and Daniel lay sprawled on the deck, motionless under the blanket that Elsie had thrown over him when she realised that he had fallen asleep while they were talking.

She smiled to herself as contentment unexpectedly washed over her. They had caught more fish earlier today, two fine pollock, and her belly was full. With this easy wind, they planned to sail on as long as it would take them, and while her body was stiff and cold, she felt calm and full of purpose as their boat slipped on through the silvery night.

She and Daniel had talked for many hours today. He had asked her, tentatively, what she hoped to achieve from meeting her mother and she'd answered, looking at him with a face full of such honesty that he had felt his heart break a little more, even when he thought he couldn't feel any more grief after the loss of his father.

'Nothing,' she replied, bluntly. 'But I do need to see her and tell her what happened. And that we don't need her now.'

He had nodded, understanding. Elsie had learnt to cope without her father, just as he had, and her mother had had no contact for years. She owed her nothing, and although she had no need to accept her back into her very self-sufficient life, the pull of a mother figure in an otherwise orphaned future was very strong, nonetheless. Elsie needed to see her, that much was plain.

Whether she chose to begin a new relationship with her was quite another.

She squinted ahead as she let her mind wander, searching her memory for her early childhood and elusive glimpses of her mother. If she was honest, she was unsure now which memories were real and which were created in her more wishful daydreams. Her solid memories were full of Dad and Jack, her heart lurching painfully as she thought of Jack receiving her letter, perhaps alone, but surely afraid and homesick. She did remember her mum holding the back of her coat while she leant over the quay to scrutinise the little fishing line Dad had given her for her birthday, laughter and squeals as she reeled in the crafty crabs who always dropped back in as she lifted them clear of the water. She scowled again as she tried to see more, but it seemed to her now that these dreams were all wiped out with the clarity of her memory of the night her mother left.

Elsie straightened her back and altered her course slightly, feeling the answering surge as the boat surfed onwards with the swell behind her.

Closer now, relentlessly closer, both to her destination and to the questions she was burning to ask.

***

It took them a week.

A week that Elsie thought would never end, a week where their own strength, as well as the strength of their friendship was tested.

Brutally tested, but not found wanting. The two of them raising each other's spirits from the depth of despair, if one was down, the other rallied, and it was this bond of companionship and understanding, as much as their sailing and navigational capabilities, which brought them safely into Ramsgate eight nights after slipping their lines in Christchurch.

As they made fast to the heavy iron cleats inside the harbour wall, Daniel caught the eye of one of the fishermen mending his nets on the edge of the quay.

'Not local?' he grunted. 'Fishermen, though?'

'Yes, we are,' replied Daniel, trying to inject as much firmness into his voice as he could manage. 'Not fishing here, though, we're looking for someone. Then off back to Christchurch in the next couple of days, maybe?' He hazarded a guess, glancing at Elsie for confirmation, and getting his answer from her emphatic nod.

'She'll be safe enough here,' said the man. His brusque manner belied by the softness in his eyes when he saw how young Elsie was, and how Daniel was limping. 'There's a guesthouse up that way' – he nodded – 'does a fine dinner and not too pricey either,' he added.

Thanking him effusively, the two of them tidied the boat, then slinging their bags over their shoulders, they went ashore, astonished to find how uncertain their legs were now they were back on dry land. Elsie eyed Daniel, worriedly. He was limping badly and leaning hard on his crutches, trying not to wince as he put weight on his bad leg, but he returned her look with a dismissive scowl.

'It's just stiff,' he said, 'too long sitting on deck and no exercise.'

Elsie let it go, knowing partly that he was right and also that he needed space from her concern while he tried to limber back up. She fell in beside him as they walked away from the quay, and both were enormously relieved when the next passer-by, an elderly woman with inquisitive eyes, confirmed that they were headed in the right direction for a bed for the night.

**

Elsie woke with a start. She had been dreaming, confused,

disturbing dreams, where Dad's face kept getting mixed up with Daniel's, and all the time knowing that she had to find something important that she couldn't place. Dad and Daniel telling her to leave it, Jack's voice drifting into her consciousness and ordering her, like the soldier he now was, to carry on regardless.

She shivered and rolled over, jumped when she realised that Daniel was on the rug on the floor next to her bed. She looked down at him guiltily, grateful that he had seen her fatigue and offered her the bed, even though he probably needed comfort more than she, his twisted leg throbbing despite using the crutches he despised so much.

Trying not to wake him, she slid carefully out of bed and tiptoed over to the window, peeling the blackout carefully back and letting the grey early morning light flood the room.

It was a dreary looking day, drizzle streaking the windowpane and obscuring her view of the street below. Her mother's address from the top of the letter was ingrained in her mind, yet she went to her bag to check it again. Her eyes lingered over the words her mother had written in painstakingly blotted ink.

'...I know you are probably surprised to hear from me after all this time. I am sorry about Dad and I promise I will do everything I can to help. I would love to see my son and daughter again. I do miss you both so much...'

I do miss you. Elsie scowled ferociously. So why was this the first time she'd heard of it?

'You always scare me when you look like that,' Daniel said, and Elsie jumped and laughed at the sound of his voice.

'Breakfast,' she announced, firmly. 'Then I need to find her. Today.'

But as they arrived at the top end of Chapel Road, a pencilled map from their voluble landlady clutched in her damp palm, her courage failed her and she stopped so abruptly that Daniel cannoned into her, bumping her painfully with a crutch as he fought to retrieve his balance. They apologised at the same time, then both burst into nervous laughter. Daniel caught hold of her hand and squeezed it hard as he saw tears starting in Elsie's eyes.

'Are you sure you want to do this?' he asked and Elsie nodded.

'I just have to, Daniel,' she said simply.

When they reached the scuffed wooden door, he saw her hesitate again, wanted to knock for her but stopped himself. This was Elsie's path, he couldn't rush her into this, in fact, he wanted her to walk away now, afraid she would be hurt beyond repair by the woman who had once deserted her.

Then Elsie stepped forward and they both held their breath as the sharp rap on the knocker reverberated in the quiet of the morning. Listened to the footsteps scuffling inside, then the door swinging cautiously open, an eye peering round. Then the door swinging wide as a woman, an older version and the spitting image of Elsie stood there, her hand flying to her mouth in shock as the tears came from mother and daughter alike.

Daniel took one look at their faces, identical hazel eyes framed by a mop of curls, and cleared his throat, quietly.

'I'll come back later, Elsie.'

Neither woman heard as he turned away, his crutches tap-tapping as he limped back up the street, utterly alone.

***

Elsie heard the door click behind her as her mother led her down the little hall into the kitchen. Her eyes flitted around the room, incredulously noted the similarity in some of the curtains and cushions scattered on the wooden chairs, realising that the kitchen that she'd inherited as her mother walked out was still her mother's taste and choice and was mirrored here, many, many nautical miles away in Ramsgate.

The same, but different. A little wooden highchair at the kitchen table, and as her mind reeled, her mother bent and picked up the little girl who had been sitting there, turning to face Elsie with wary eyes.

'Yours?' Elsie faltered, after a long pause, and then saw shock in her mother's face.

'You didn't know?'

'How could I possibly have known? You left, remember? I didn't even know you were still alive until you wrote when Dad passed.' Elsie's sudden fury left her as her voice broke over her last words, and suddenly tears were running down her face, unchecked.

And as the little girl also burst in sobs at the angry words spattering across the kitchen, warm arms went around Elsie, the scent and the comfort so familiar to her that she gasped and instinctively returned the embrace, the two women clutching at each other with the child between them as the storm passed over.

Much later, they sat at the table, Elsie nursing a cup of tea and watching curiously as her mother passed food tidbits to the little girl, this tiny half-sister, undreamt of until today.

'Actually, I wrote to Bill all the time,' said her mother, quietly. 'I always hoped we could make things better. I never wanted to leave, but I couldn't stay with things how they were. And when I met Jim, I told Bill because I truly hoped he might fight for me, but he never wrote back. I haven't been in touch for a few years now, but when Daisy was born, I had to tell him, I thought you had a right to know. She was a bit of a happy accident, actually' – she blushed to the roots of her hair – 'to be honest I thought I was too old.'

Elsie blushed, too. 'He never said anything,' she answered eventually, her eyes fixed on the curly little head, chubby little hands reaching into the bowl to eat the last tasty morsels, black eyelashes fanned above the curve of her tiny cheek and her eyes ever watchful.

Betsy sighed.

'He wasn't much of a talker, your dad,' she said, 'and when he stopped fishing, he just seemed to stop in his tracks, somehow. It seemed to me the war never really ended for some of us.'

Elsie kept her eyes down, a little spurt of anger flaring within her.

'Maybe you should have talked to him more.' She burst out, suddenly unable to contain herself. 'He talked to me. He went to sea and rescued Daniel, and he talked to me.'

She stopped abruptly as Daisy broke into a wail at the sound of her raised voice and hung her head in shame when Betsy glared at her reprovingly.

'You've no right to tell me that I should have talked more,' she snapped back. 'I looked after that man, and I cooked and cleaned for him, and I might never have even existed. The hours I spent on that house, on our marriage and all for nothing, until now.'

Betsy broke off suddenly, biting her tongue and her face flaming. Elsie looked up sharply, felt a chill go through her, just as surely as if there had been an actual drop in temperature.

'What do you mean, "until now"?' she asked icily and watched as her mother shifted uncomfortably.

'I meant nothing much,' she replied, not meeting Elsie's glare. 'Except, of course, it's my house now that Bill's gone.'

Elsie's mouth went dry, and at the same moment she felt her heart thudding uncomfortably in her chest.

'Yours?' she managed. 'But you live here. You have your life and I have mine. Jack and I don't need you any more.'

Betsy stared at her, trying to find the right words to retrieve the situation which had gone so suddenly downhill, from mother and daughter embracing to a pair of lionesses pacing uneasily around a kill.

'I mean, now that there's a war on, it makes more sense for us girls to live together, look after each other,' she said, carefully, watching for Elsie's reaction.

'So where is he?' asked Elsie abruptly, realising as she spoke that she knew nothing about this man, Jim, the man who had stolen her mother away, who could claim to be her stepfather, and the father of the whimpering toddler huddled on her mother's lap. 'Volunteered, did he?'

Again, the shifty look. Elsie frowned as her mother looked down, seemingly to compose herself before she spoke again. 'He went to France,' she said. 'I haven't heard from him in a while.' And suddenly, Elsie knew beyond all doubt that she was lying. Buying time to think of a response, using the simplest trick of wartime to explain away a missing husband.

'You left him too, didn't you,' she flared, and as her mother's face went crimson, she knew she'd been right. 'You've left him, or he's thrown you out, and you want to take our house for yourself.'

As Betsy half-rose from her chair, excuses springing from her lips, Elsie stood too, pushing her chair back so suddenly that it fell backwards and crashed to the floor. As Daisy burst into fresh sobs of terror, she pushed her mother's suddenly grasping hands away from her as she stepped towards the door.

'Go to her,' she spat. 'She needs you. We don't.'

And with her eyes blinded by hot, contemptuous tears, she span on her heel and slammed her way out of the door.

***

Elsie ran.

Scuttling out of the door, shoving her mother's greedy hands away, she put her head down and ran. Tears blinding her as she turned the corner at the end of the street, she tripped over something by her feet, strong hands steadying her and preventing her flight. She struggled briefly, then, completely spent, leant into the familiar scent that smelt of home, friendship and security.

Daniel had been waiting for her, and the tears fell unchecked as she realised just how long he must have been sitting there. All those hours while she'd sat holding her little sister and drinking tea, drinking in her mother's sweet deception, her dear friend had waited faithfully, despite the cold eating into his crippled leg, wary of what she might discover and unwilling to leave her to face it alone.

Elsie collapsed against him, the relief at finding his strong arms around her turning her anger and betrayal into hot, bitter tears.

'She just wants the house,' she managed eventually. 'She's down on her luck and she wants my house.'

Daniel stared at her desolate face, aghast. Memories of his own, close family threatened to overwhelm him as he realised the depths of the hurt that Elsie was now feeling. Anger welled up and he hugged her fiercely.

'Let's get out of here, she doesn't deserve you,' he muttered into her dark curls, still holding her tight, and feeling her struggle, he looked down into her wet eyes.

'It's not just her,' she said, bleakly. 'It seems I have a sister now too. Everyone seems to have someone, but Dad's dead and Jack's gone to war.'

And with that, she became unable to speak further, and, slipping his arm through hers, Daniel retrieved his crutch and the two friends limped back to the guest house, mortally wounded in body and soul.

***

Daniel suddenly stirred, and not sure why he had woken so abruptly, rubbed the sleep from his eyes and sat up to check on Elsie. Seeing her bed was empty, he reached for his crutch and hauled himself upright, cursing silently that he was unable to do this without assistance from his wooden companion, nor with any grace. As he stood, he stiffened when he realised that Elsie was sitting on the floor with her back to the wall, tears coursing noiselessly down her cheeks, her hands twisting savagely in her lap.

'Elsie?' he said and stumped carefully over to her side of the room.

Elsie looked up and offered a watery grin.

'I'm actually sadder about not getting to know my sister,' she said, quietly. 'My mum left me years ago, but it's strange knowing that little Daisy is there, and I won't get to be part of her life.'

Daniel thought carefully before he answered. Elsie seemed so brittle and what mattered to him most was that his friend knew that she was loved.

'You could come back,' he said, ignoring her shaking head. 'You could give it some time and come back to visit Daisy. Your mum might not like it, but I think you have a right to see her. And anyway,' he added, 'your mum might get to realise what she gave up when she walked out on you like that.'

'Do you think she could take the house away?' asked Elsie trying as hard as she could to keep her voice steady.

'I just don't know,' answered Daniel, honestly. 'I think you need to talk to your dad's solicitor, see what was said exactly in the letter that was sent to her when he passed on. It might actually belong to you and Jack, for all you know.'

Elsie nodded, firmly, feeling a sense of purpose coming back, and she smiled gratefully at Daniel.

'What I really want to do now is get the boat provisioned and get sailing again,' she stated. 'I don't know if Jack ever got my letter, and I want to go home and make sure I'm there waiting for him when he gets back from France.'

***

Within the hour, they had packed their meagre belongings and went downstairs to check out of the little guest house. To their surprise, however, the landlady appeared wild eyed and distracted, and was barely able to add up their little bill.

'Are you all right, Miss?' ventured Daniel, and she glared at him.

'Haven't you heard? On the wireless?' she demanded. 'Our boys are stuck in France. We're readying the boats to go and save them all. It's been all over the wireless, Mr Churchill himself is calling for boats, God rest him.' And with that, she burst into tears.

'Is Mr Churchill dead, then?' wondered Elsie bemused, and their landlady sobbed harder.

'No, that's me being all overcome.' She sniffed. 'But he's called for boats to help bring our boys back, and I'm off to the quay to see who's come to help.' And with that, she turned on her heel and stalked out of the door, her back stiff with duty but her shoulders trembling, nonetheless.

Elsie and Daniel stared at each other. Bright spots danced suddenly before Elsie's eyes, and suddenly she felt her legs buckling as Daniel's arms enfolded her, for the second time in as many days.

'Jack.' She breathed. 'Jack's in danger.'

'Elsie, we have to get home, we have to get home NOW and get ready to look after him.' Daniel shook Elsie gently, shocked at the wide, vacant pupils in her ashen face. 'ELSIE!!! We have to go, love.'

With that, he counted out what was due for the room for the past few nights and left it under the little 'welcome' sign on the table by the front door. Taking Elsie's hand to steady her, he slung his pack over his other shoulder, and awkwardly went to pick up his crutch, clicking his tongue with exasperation as it clattered to the floor. Elsie came to at the sound, her face filling with – Daniel looked away and bit his tongue – filling with pity.

'Let's go' he repeated, and Elsie took up her own pack and loosed Daniel's hand so he could manage his own.

When they reached the quay, they both stopped stock still, taken aback by the scene before them.

Boats. Big boats, little boats, fishing boats, and pleasure boats, all moored side by side like sardines in the little port. Men scurrying around making ready, the scene was that of purpose and speed. Elsie shivered; she could sense another feeling, a sharp, pervasive fear, a dread that they may already be too late.

There was no way they could leave. Daniel's boat was moored beside the quay, completely hemmed in by boats alongside, as well as fore and aft.

'We aren't going anywhere soon, he observed bleakly, but his words drew little response from the girl at his side, and he glanced sideways to see her face. And stiffened at what he saw there, almost, almost, allowing himself an inward smile at what he knew would be her answer, but silenced by the magnitude of what this would mean for them both.

'Oh yes we are,' she said. 'We're going with them.'

Part 2

Monique

CHAPTER 10

On the Farm… *A la ferme*: 1940

Monique paused for a moment, leaning her hot forehead against the flank of the cow she was milking. Breathing in its sweet, musty smell, she shut her eyes, the sounds of the other cows jostling gently in the barn soothing her.

She was bone weary. She had risen at five, this morning and every morning, for as long as she could remember. Since Maman died, in fact, but her mind clanged shut as she thought of that, and she raised her head sharply, spooking the cow before her with her sudden movement.

'Shhh, girl,' she murmured, and the cow quietened, trusting the calm authority of the young woman moving purposefully through the barn, morning and night for the last decade, to get the milking done.

It was no good. In the warmth of the early sunrise, her hands working methodically under each cow in turn, her mind slid inexorably back to the night when she lost her mother.

Dad had not come back from the war. Monique was conceived during his last leave from the trenches, and never laid eyes on the gaunt young man who Maman had talked about, late into the night as they cuddled together under thick flannel sheets in the bed they had shared since she'd been born in it. Maman used to hold her and smile at her memories, then, as Monique was lulled into sleep, she would feel her thin shoulders shuddering with sobs and would roll closer, reaching her little arms around her mother to give her comfort, mother and daughter mourning what one had lost and the other had never known.

As Monique grew older, if anything, they had grown closer. Maman had been a governess in England before she'd married her father and had an almost impeccable grasp of the language. Although Monique went to the local *primaire*, by the time she went to the *lycee*, Maman seemed to need her more and more on the farm, and she began to go in late on some days and leave early on others. As they walked the cows back from the field to the barn, their feet growing dusty in the cow's wake, Maman would begin to speak in English, pointing out flowers and trees and giving the English names, so that, gradually, the names of the French flowers and trees, *chene* and oak, *amandiers* and almond, *saule* and willow, would blend together in a gentle, sun-touched melange as their dusty feet scuffed the scorched grass and bees bumbled drunkenly across the vast delicacy of the ripe sunflowers swaying heavily on the hot breeze.

Her cough had not been noticeable at first. Her first real symptoms were back pain, deep, intractable pain making Lisette toss and turn all night, bathed in sweat and pale with exhaustion as the weeks went by. By the time the cough began, she'd already been to her doctor, to be told what she'd already guessed, that her slender frame was wracked with tuberculosis, ingested breath by breath and with each glass of warm milk from the cows which were their very livelihood.

As each day passed, Monique took over the milking, but as each night passed, there was nothing she could do but to watch helplessly and hold her mother up to help her to cough free the mucus that was choking her every breath.

On the last night, Lisette lay quietly, at first, gritting her teeth against the pain slicing through her spine. Her eyes followed Monique around the room, watching the girl washing her face and slipping into her nightgown, each movement precise and careful not to make a noise that might disturb her beloved mother.

Monique suddenly felt the weight of Lisette's stare and turned, smiling tiredly as their eyes met. Without a word, Lisette stretched out her wasted arms, and Monique rushed into them, the tears coming as she returned her mother's embrace. As the coughing began, she felt the weakness of Lisette's frame, surely unable to stand another night of her bones being wracked by this shattering, internal force, her body's last effort to cast out this terrible disease. Monique felt her own heart breaking as her mother's broken body shuddered and arced in pain, 'shhh Maman, shhhh now,' she murmured, over and over, as she had done every night for weeks now.

And suddenly, finally, it was quiet.

Monique came awake, her ears straining to hear what might have woken her, until the realisation struck her that it was the complete absence of sound from the frail form on the other side of the bed.

The enormity of the utter silence hit her abruptly and she sat up, frantically tugging at the bunched-up blankets to see her mother's calm, dead, face. Kneeling to lean over her and pressing her lips against her mother's still-warm lips, breathing her own breath into her unresponsive lungs again and again and again, until finally, she sat back on her haunches and saw, for the first time, that her mother was in a place of complete peace. The pain gone; the sickness ended. Monique sat and stared, hearing the sound of her own last breath slipping from her mother's lips, and knew that it was over.

Monique had no idea what to do. At sixteen years old, she had no one to turn to, had spent the last few years increasingly involved with the farm instead of with school and friends. True to her upbringing, she covered her mother's face and went to milk the cows.

Reality had hit when she returned from the milking shed. Monique stood, frozen by the silence in the sunny farm kitchen, the lack of life belied by the dancing of dust motes in the sunlight. She fell apart then, utterly unable to walk up the stairs to where her mother's body lay, she dropped to her knees, an animalic wailing keening from her lips as tears blinded her, rocking back and forth with her hands pressed to her hot face, barely aware, sometime later that there was someone else there, kind hands under her arms raising her to her feet, cold water put to her lips and a rug around her shaking shoulders.

It was the farmer's wife from the neighbouring farm, who had first heard the frantic lowing of the cattle desperate to be let out to the fields, for Monique, in her dazed state, had milked them but not thrown the latch on the barn door to allow them to roam free and graze. Solange had heard the sound on the breeze and had guessed immediately what had happened, Lisette's plight had become increasingly obvious and the whole village had been holding its breath. Barking orders at her husband to ring for the village doctor, she'd run as fast as she could to help the stricken girl, but as her husband joined her with the doctor, her face fell as she saw the vet standing behind them.

'I had no choice, cherie,' muttered her husband, his face darkening with shame and his lips trembling with distress. 'It's tuberculosis, we all know it. The cattle will have to be inspected, I'm so sorry, Monique.'

Monique heard his words as if through a fog. The words meant nothing and everything, her heart and her mind utterly unable to reconcile the events unfolding before her eyes.

In the end, half the cattle were slaughtered. The neighbours sheltered Monique as best as they could, but nothing could have stopped her hearing the shots ringing out and the thuds of her beloved cows falling to the ground. The half that were not infected were moved out to the fields, allowing the neighbours finally to feel they could help Monique in some tangible way, assisting with the disinfection of the barn and milking shed in line with the new laws, even helping her sign the forms the vet gave her to apply for compensation.

Compensation.

Monique's mouth twisted bitterly at the memory, as if forty per cent compensation for the lost animals and milk could make up for that time of anguish. What price her mother's life? What price the loneliness and the decisions of having to run the farm alone, cutting back to the bare bones to run at a profit but without it becoming too much for her to work alone? Countless nights sitting up balancing the books by candlelight, not daring to use any of the precious fuel she was saving for winter, wondering time and again if she could simply live out her days as a smallholding, not selling her produce at market but just feeding herself directly from the farm. Realising then that she would go mad without outside contact, that her regular customers buying her milk and cheeses at the market were helping her stay human, stopping her from descending a slippery path into an abject hand to mouth existence.

She needed to do more than just survive.

Her cheeses were already good, but Monique discovered that she had a way with butter, churning out creamy pats that the villages bought by the pound. And one sweet, sweet day, her neighbour, Solange introduced her to beekeeping.

Whether it was the humming she found soothing, or the slow, deliberate movements that Solange advised, Monique found the process of settling the bees into the hive, caring for them and eventually harvesting their sweet honey was almost meditative, soothing her in the same way that milking did, and as she carefully extracted the honeycombs she found herself murmuring the English words for what she was doing under her breath in a steady drone, just as her mother had always done. 'Honey, *miele*. Calm, *calme*. Steady, *sage*.'

The bees thrived, and Monique found she wanted to know more and more about her busy charges.

'Madame?' she ventured one day, and Solange looked up in surprise, as Monique was normally very reserved and rarely chatted as they worked. 'The honey is good, but it is seasonal. Can you teach me how to use the beeswax? I need to keep the market stall going this winter.' And as she said it, her shoulders shivered suddenly at the thought of the dark months ahead. The summer was in full swing, but she knew she had to make plans, and as soon as possible to get through the colder months alone.

Solange put her hands on her ample hips and blew through her breath through her teeth as she thought.

'I used to do it, but it's been a long time,' she admitted. 'I've turned more to helping Armand on the farm and spend less time with the bees these days, but I'll have a look at my old diaries and try to remember.'

Weeks went by, and Monique became so busy with potting up her honey and butter for the stall in the simmering summer heat that she all but forgot about the conversation and the inevitable onslaught of winter. Until one day, she was standing at her stall shading her eyes from the blinding sun, when a shadow fell across her and she shivered as if winter had suddenly struck. She blinked. The shadow moved and materialised into Solange, who had become increasingly dear to her over the past few weeks, and she was beaming.

'Here you are, ma cherie,' she said triumphantly, holding out a worn little notebook held together with a twist of leather. 'Welcome to the world of beeswax.'

Monique opened the book and her eyes opened wide in awe at what she saw. Meticulously depicted in a series of tight scribbles and pencilled diagrams, were instructions for extracting beeswax from the hive, but more than this, there were recipes, countless detailed recipes describing beeswax polish, soap, candles, and more.

'This is wonderful, Madame,' she said, and tears pricked her eyes when Solange leant over to embrace her, her loneliness suddenly overwhelming her with the older woman's kindness.

Oh, how she missed Maman. The emptiness of the bed next to her helped her rise early every morning, unwilling to spend time dwelling on her loss. The cows anchored her to routine, but more and more her interest in the bees helped her look to the future which had otherwise yawned emptily ahead.

Night after night, she hunched over the battered little book, her lips forming each word as she read, tying the leather thong around it reverently after each reading to protect it against the messy detritus from her increasingly bold experiments.

One night, she knocked excitedly on Solange's door. She had been working steadily on a new project and was ready to share this with her friend – beautiful and long-lasting candles, the scent of sweet beeswax filling her home as she worked on each new batch which she intended to start marketing as soon as the weather turned a bit colder in the autumn.

She knocked again, impatient now, listening for a stirring within. When there was nothing, she stepped back, puzzled, looking at the window for a sign of life.

What she saw turned her cold with fear.

Solange was sitting slumped at the table, her head buried in her hands, completely still. Her own hands shaking, Monique reached out and unlatched the kitchen door, and to her enormous relief, the creaking as she pushed it wide seem to stir the prostate woman, who raised swollen eyes to Monique and burst into tears afresh.

'What on Earth's happened, Madame?' Monique asked aghast at her shattered visage and all thoughts of beeswax dispelled.

'It's the bloody Bosch.' Solange wept. 'It's happening again, Monique, it's happening all over again. We're at war.'

Chapter 11

Occupation and Violation

The Germans overran the land. Within days they heard they were coming, a palpable wave of fear hitting the villagers like the cold wind before a train arriving at a platform.

'They are coming for our farms, come and stay with us and we can look after each other,' beseeched Solange, but Monique was adamant that she would remain at home.

She couldn't leave her mother's bed. She had been born there, and Maman had died there. Leaving here was not an option, and the young woman rose and descended to the milk shed each morning with stiff resolve in her gait despite the dread in her heart.

That morning was no different. Memories of Maman and the night she died kept resurfacing today, however, and Monique found herself shaking her head angrily to keep her thoughts on the job, inadvertently startling the cows each time she did so. The meditative calm that normally fell upon her was elusive today, perhaps it was the gossip she knew would be rife at the market today, she mused, briefly to herself, then focussed her mind back on the job.

She needed to get finished. She wanted to check on the bees first, but she knew that the market would be buzzing louder with talk of the Bosch. They were everywhere now, the men sullenly ducking from their gaze, the women curious but afraid of these sharply dressed and even sharper speaking men who had taken over this country and this town.

Something clattered in the yard outside and she started at the sound, raising her forehead from the cow's flank once again and shaking drops of warm milk from her hands.

Footsteps. She straightened up and waited silently, knowing that it wouldn't be her neighbours, Solange and Armand would already have called a greeting so as not to alarm her.

They came closer, louder now and lots of them. Galvanised into action, she sprang back behind the cow which was skittering nervously now with the milk sloshing in the pail beneath her legs, her eyes searching for the metal loop which would raise the trap door to the level below where she stored all her beeswax in the cool cellar beneath the milking shed. Grasping it and slipping her slender form through the gap as quickly and as quietly as she was able, painfully aware of her breath rasping in and out of her terrified lungs.

They had come for her farm.

***

She was too late. There was nowhere to truly hide from these soldiers, the efficiency of their search bringing them ever closer.

As she lay on her back in the low space, almost completely filled with crates of beeswax, its sweet smell cloying suddenly in the back of her throat, she saw the latch move again, saw the hatch rise and the faces leering down at her.

Alien voices, harsh commands which she did not understand but which her body tried, against her will, to obey.

Climbing back up and being wrenched to her feet as she emerged, fingers jabbing and voices accusing. The cows becoming agitated as the soldiers pushed past them, boys really, some part of her mind thought, boys in stiff uniforms and even sterner anger.

She did not understand their words, but she understood their intent when they began passing up her crates of carefully stashed candles, her jars of beeswax leather polish, her face creams scented with the very essence of the flowers of her fields, lovingly made and meticulously stored ready for the winter markets. Every last crate, plundered. Every product touched with their grubby, grasping fingers, and suddenly Monique could bear it no more.

She put her head down and ran straight at them, aware that she was screaming and seeing the shock in the face of the leader as he turned to grab her wrists, forcing her hands down and away so that she couldn't scratch at his face as she'd intended. Pushing her hard, and then to her horror and shame, reaching down to lift her ankles from the ground, forcing her to fall backwards into the waiting arms of the other men.

Screaming. White hot pain, again and again and again. The weight of their bodies on her, her spine grinding into the dirt. The blood beginning to seep into the dusty floorboards, forming a dark stain beneath her motionless form. The sound of a harsh voice shouting 'Halt, genug,' but barely registering where this voice was coming from, was it from the man still straining on top of her, or was it the one poking at her ribs with his booted foot?

Suddenly, weightless, the man grinning above her yanked up by an older man, was this the man doing all the shouting, she wondered, hazily?

She wished the shouting would stop. In fact, she wished it would all stop, and she found herself humming, forcing all other sounds and feelings out of her mind with her tuneless notes. The sound anchored her, the droning so familiar that she could switch off the scene before her eyes and see something else, in fact, was that her own mother she could see?

'Maman?' she wondered, entranced, sure that she could see her, actually see her standing beside the first beehive. Pointing at it. Winking slyly, just a little gesture between mother and daughter, all that was required in this time of great need.

Part of her watched the older man shouting, part of her shuddered as the younger men (five of them? Six?), began pulling up their trousers and hastily buttoning their flies. The other part watching Maman, knowing what she had to do, knowing that Lisette would surely help her.

In one fluid movement, she rolled, fast as a snake, almost faltering as Maman disappeared, but nonetheless flipping the lid open on the first and then the second beehive, kicking them hard and watching in satisfaction as the bees swarmed furiously towards the movement all around them. The movement of fleeing men, beating at their own heads, eyes and ears filled with insects bent on revenge, rendering them blind and deaf, insensible to everything except the need to rid themselves of the buzzing and the stings.

Monique watched until the last man had gone, noting absently that one had soiled himself in his panic, that another had screamed like a child.

Then the dust motes span in the hot sun and her legs gave way as, blessedly, oblivion claimed her.

***

Soft voices wakened her.

Monique opened her eyes a crack, watching without moving, unsure of where she was and afraid beyond fear that the soldiers might have come back.

A sob of relief caught in her throat as she recognised Solange, her sturdy frame encased in a floury apron as she worked over her hot stove. Solange heard the sound escaping from the battered girl resting on the mattress on the kitchen floor and whirled to look at her, then in the next motion, she gestured her husband out of the room, and all Monique saw was his retreating back as he left, hurriedly.

Her eyes filled with tears. Despite the trauma she'd just endured, she was quite able to make the distinction between the greedy clutching hands of the German soldiers and the kindly features of Armand, her old friend. And then Solange was leaning over and stroking her matted hair back from her forehead, murmuring softly as the sobs engulfed her, shaking her slight frame, and rendering her unable to speak.

Hours seemed to pass, time flowing without measure as Solange heated pails of water and began to fill the tin bath by the stove. Sponging her bruised body gently and holding her hair back when she vomited at the sight of the blood on her own thighs. Shushing her sobs but at the same time, allowing her to weep unchecked, teasing a comb through her tangled hair and washing out the dirt and caked blood where she must have hit her head on the floorboards.

'The bees?' she wondered and wept again when Solange shook her head.

'They have gone, cherie,' she answered. 'But I'm thinking they did a good job for you, no?'

Monique forced her mind back to the events in the milking shed to try to recall exactly what had happened, but her mind clanged shut then, a black shutter coming down to protect her from images too fresh and too bloody to contemplate.

When her body was clean, she rested back, utterly exhausted, on the mattress, and Solange sat down and took her hands. 'I must call a doctor, cherie,' she said, quietly, and squeezed her hands firmly when Monique began to shake her head frantically. 'I will send for the sage-femme, Monique. You are old enough to bleed, and we must not let these pigs leave their mark.'

And while Monique sobbed and protested, terrified that this woman would need to undress her, examine her, she leant out into the yard and called her husband, but although shy in the ways of women, Armand was a farmer, born and bred, and had had the presence of mind to send for the sage-femme, who was already in the yard and jumping down from her old pony trap.

Her experienced eye and calm presence calmed her, and in the end, Monique was able to swallow the bitter tisane which the woman brewed, assuring her that she need not worry.

'All of this will pass, child,' she murmured gently, and lulled by the soporific warmth of the stove and a strange floating sensation she began to feel after she'd drunk the last dregs, Monique shut her eyes and was almost able to believe her.

Chapter 12

Retribution

The next day, Monique woke with a start, and lay for a few moments trying to orientate herself. As the sunlight streamed in, her eyes fell on Solange, once again standing over her stove and stirring some concoction that smelt so good, Monique's empty stomach growled. As she sat up, the ache between her thighs shocked her and she had to catch her breath, the sound causing Solange to turn to her with a worried frown.

'How are you today, ma petite?' she asked gently, and once again, Monique's eyes filled with ready tears.

'I'm all right,' she lied, and levered herself up to give Solange a watery smile. 'And thank you. Thank you for coming to help me.' She bit her lip, not wanting to look back to the events of the day before.

Solange leant over to envelope her in a floury hug, and for a moment, Monique allowed herself to sink into the embrace, and then missing her mother so acutely that she was almost unable to breathe, she pulled away and gasped.

'I'm sorry. I have to go.'

'Go?' asked Solange, confusion all over her kindly face. 'The cows have been milked, Monique. The bees have flown. You need to rest, child.'

Monique shook her head, struggling up out of the blankets and climbing gingerly to her feet. Her head swam for a moment, and she paused, it would be so easy to sink back down and be cared for, nurtured in a way that her young soul missed so dreadfully.

But she knew she had to go. Her home was waiting for her, and the vision that she'd had the day before of her mother danced before her eyes, calling her back to her home and the bed she'd slept in since the day she was born.

'I just have to go,' she said facing Solange, and her neighbour sighed, knowing that the girl needed to feel safe in her own home, but that she was unlikely to feel this way when she was alone.

'Eat first, child,' she said, brusquely. 'Eat and then get back home. Me and Armand will come in and check on you tonight,' and she noticed how the girls' eyes flickered with relief at this.

In the end, they were too late.

***

Monique walked into her yard and bolted the gate, leaning against the sun-warmed wood and letting her tears run, oblivious to them dripping down her face and from her chin.

Relief that she was at home and able to let go, combined with trepidation at how she might feel when she had to step inside the milking shed in the morning. Her eyes taking in the open beehives, empty now, a greater service rendered than she'd ever hoped for when she began to study their busy way of life, and for a moment, she allowed herself a tight smile when she thought of the soldiers running and screaming when the swarms had descended upon them. Then her face hardened when she remembered her plundered stocks, her precious candles and beeswax creams stolen from under her nose. She would have to get busy again, and fast, but she had no clear idea what to do now that the bees had gone.

She walked sadly over to the milk shed, and taking a deep breath, she pushed open the door, wincing as it creaked on its old hinges. I must oil those, she thought, anything to distract herself as she went inside, her eyes falling upon the trap door to the cellar, where thankfully Armand had swept and cleaned away the dust and bloodstains from the day before. Dust motes swam before her eyes again, but she steadied herself with a steady litany of English words again as her mother had always done. Hay…*foins*, milking pail…*seau de traite*, pitchfork…*fourche de lancement*. Her breathing grew calmer, and she went through to the back of the milking shed and out into the field, where her eyes took in the age-old scene of her cows grazing peacefully in the sunlight.

Suddenly, she heard the door hinges creak again behind her, and she started violently, called out 'Solange?' but without any real hope in her heart. She knew it wasn't Solange.

The German soldier stood before her, one hand pushing the heavy door shut behind him, the other holding a length of rope. His smile was cold, and Monique felt her knees buckling as her eyes took in his sneering face, swollen almost beyond recognition by the welts all over from the bees frenzied attack.

As he stepped towards her, he pushed her hard and she fell back towards the wall, sending something clattering to the floor beside her, and in that moment, she knew what it was and snatched it up in one fluid movement.

The man grunted once, then looked down at his chest and back up at her, the shock on his face almost making her feel sorry for him as his fingers plucked uselessly at the prongs of the pitchfork sunk deep into his chest.

'*Forche de lancement*, pitchfork,' she whispered, savagely, and as the blood began to froth from his mouth with his last breaths, Monique backed away out into the field. Whispering goodbye to the home she'd known all her life, goodbye to her childhood, and goodbye to the place where she'd nursed her mother to her grave, she turned swiftly and walked away, not knowing particularly where she was going, but knowing that she was never, ever coming back.

Part 3

Josef

CHAPTER 13

The End of Dreams: 1939

Josef sighed, blinked his eyes hard against the glare of the gaslight on the book he was studying, then gave up and closed his heavy lids. Tiredness overwhelmed him and he sat quietly, giving up to the moment and letting sleep take him.

He had been working so hard. The hiss of the gaslight, a harsh sound yet so familiar as to be soothing, lulled him deeper into sleep, and the crash of the front door sent him to his feet in an instant, his head spinning and his heart pounding in shock.

'Josef? Josef, it's Mutti, where are you?'

Josef pressed his hands hard over his heart, willing it to calm down. 'Up here, Mutti,' he called, noting the tremor in his voice, the tremor that had been there since his father had been taken.

That night, the door had crashed open so violently that his mother had been thrown back against the wall, and Josef had sat, rocking back and forth in the kitchen with his hands pressed over his ears, too afraid to make a sound, too afraid to move. Too afraid to try to help, but worst of all, too afraid to say goodbye to his father, who had been taken from them that night while his mother railed and screamed at the men in the black shirts.

They had been civil to her, but they had beaten his father as he tried to protest, physically beaten his gentle, peaceable father. Hans had been injured in the Great War, injured so badly that he was unable to walk without an ugly metal frame which rubbed his hands raw with the strain of holding his weight.

He was a history teacher in the local gymnasium, and his lessons had come to the attention of the blackshirts by the whisperings of some of the other boys. Lessons preaching humility, lessons preaching justice. Lessons which were not considered desirable nor acceptable by the current regime, and the ever-vigilant Hitler Youth had self-righteously reported him to their parents, duly rewarded for their tale-telling and losing the finest history teacher they could ever had had, if only they could have listened to his heartfelt words instead of besmirching them with their own bitterness and intolerance.

Any loud noise now rendered Josef almost insensible, the banging of a door, the snapping of a twig sending shockwaves through his wiry frame, to be replaced by an aching, implacable grief as he was reminded of his loss at every sound.

He pulled himself up, sharply then, knowing that the silence his mother was listening to was equally as painful as the noise that had jarred him so badly. He painted a bright smile on his face, ran downstairs and gave her a hug. His heart hurt to see her careworn face; she must have aged a decade since his father had been taken.

'Josef,' she murmured into his chest, still surprised that her only child now towered above her, 'Josef what have you been doing? You look so tired.'

He pulled away and grimaced. 'The exams are soon, Mutti,' he replied. 'I must pass well, you know I want to go to university.'

Frieda smiled; she did indeed know what drove her son. Like father like son, his thirst for history was insatiable, and he desired nothing more than to teach like his father had. 'Does' she corrected herself automatically, she had to believe that Hans was coming home someday, although there had been no word, none whatsoever since the night he had been dragged away before her eyes.

She was so proud of Josef, but at the same time, deeply afraid that his historical interest would render him politically active, get him noticed in a way she fervently wished Hans had never dared.

But then again, none of them had ever, truly believed that neighbour would turn on neighbour, friend upon friend. That Gertrud, the mother of young Karl, whom she'd known since their babies were toddling, innocently naked on her lawn in the summer times of a simpler childhood, had turned Hans in for his beliefs, beliefs measured and tempered by the weight of history rather than drowned in dogma, but beliefs nonetheless different to those espoused by the Nazi party.

Turned him in by a simple whisper in a more powerful ear, losing Frieda her husband and Josef his father with one spiteful, bigoted word. Ending a lifetime's friendship with the woman who had helped nurse her baby through the night when he was struck down with croup, and who, in her turn, she'd looked after when Frieda was sick with scarlet fever and unable to look after little Josef, she being too weak and Hans unable to carry him as well as walk with his frame.

Frieda had lost her husband and her friend during that dark night, and the loss and loneliness sat heavily on her shoulders. The days of trust and community were over, each neighbour scuttling off to work without catching each other's eyes, some afraid to acknowledge the other, some too guilty, others simply unwilling to use the salute which was shaking their world.

Josef refused to salute. Frieda had begged him to, terrified that he would be noticed, and he conceded that he would do so at the Hitler Youth meetings which he was obliged to attend, along with Karl, his childhood friend who had brought his world crashing down. However, he mulishly refused to do this anywhere else, preferring to keep his head down, his eyes always turning away just before he could be forced to acknowledge another.

He knew it was a dangerous game to play, but his hatred for the new regime grew with every passing day and every atrocity reported back through whispers behind doors.

The Jewish tailor, gone. The mayor, popular with all the townsfolk, gone. His father, gone. No crime committed unless speaking your mind or being a little different was a crime.

Again, Josef hugged Mutti and smiled down at her.

'Did you bring food?' he asked and she grimaced, there had been so little variety in the shops for so long that feeding her growing son was a constant challenge.

'I have sausages, and I have a cabbage,' she said, and laughed when Josef's face lit up at the first words, only to darken at the last. 'It'll fill you up,' she said firmly, and pushed him out of the way to step through into the little kitchen out the back.

She had to get it cooked and Josef fed before the start of the Youth meeting, they were becoming more and more frequent now and to be late was to be noticed. To be absent, was to be arrested.

She flicked on the gas and lit the grill.

***

The words were angry, echoing around the hall and through Josef's aching head.

It was time to take back what belonged to Germany, what belonged by rights to all Germans. It was time to end the shame of the Versailles Treaty and stop kowtowing to France, to England, to all those countries laughing behind their hands at their neighbour on her knees, revelling in her weakness and distress.

Josef blinked. The hall had fallen silent, and all eyes were upon him. Forty, maybe fifty young men, boys really, all standing to attention, all with their arms raised in the hated salute. Josef hesitated for a moment, them an image of his mother before his eyes made him jump to his feet, his arm shooting out and Heil Hitler upon his lips.

'Josef,' shouted the Reichsjugendführer, and he saluted again, more crisply than ever, the blood draining from his face as the leader pushed his own face into his.

'I'm sorry,' he stammered. 'I have a headache and felt too dizzy to stand.'

The lameness of his excuse hung for a moment in the charged air between them, then he breathed again as the leader nodded, curtly.

'You are pale,' he observed. 'Go home now, eat something.'

For a tiny moment, Josef thought he had seen something, had the man winked at him? A flicker of a movement, nothing more, but with the humanity that he seemed to be displaying, Josef suspected he could be right. He nodded, quickly, thanked him and made to go, but as he turned on his heel, a last word stopped him in his tracks.

'Karl, take him home. We need to look after our young troopers, every last one of them. Make sure he gets home safely.'

His heart sank, but he pasted on a smile and thanked the Reichsjugendführer again. He raised his eyes to Karl's who was staring at him across the hall and tried to appear as if all was well. As if he didn't know it was Karl who had reported his father, and was no doubt detailed to keep an eye lest father and son share the same ideologies.

They walked fast; the silence punctuated only by the sound of their boots clattering on the cobbles. When they reached his house, Josef paused and looked briefly at Karl, eyes not meeting.

'Thank you for coming with me.' he muttered, but Karl was not going to let it go quite so easily. To his horror, he reached past Josef and rapped hard on the door knocker, the sound making Josef start and his heart race. The sound of his mother's footsteps came from within, and when her fearful voice called out 'who is there?' his heart broke a little more. Karl pushed the door wide and smiled to see her cowering behind the door, dread in her eyes and her hands raised to ward off whatever blow might be coming her way.

Karl's beefy hand shot up and she flinched.

'Heil Hitler,' he shouted, and sneered with satisfaction when they both responded immediately, arms aloft and zeal on their lips.

When they shut the door behind them, Josef just made it to the bathroom before he vomited.

***

Six weeks later, Josef finished his exams at the gymnasium. Exhausted but elated, he half-ran home, anxious to celebrate with Mutti, whom he knew was doing her best to source some oxtail to make a stew in his honour. The results wouldn't be out for some time, but today was the last day of study, the last day of working so hard his eyes watered and his head throbbed.

He slipped his key into the front door, turning a blind eye to the paint peeling away from the old wood that his father used to strip down and repaint to be fresh with each spring. There was no paint now, the shops had been emptied of everything but basic essentials for as long as the young man could remember, but he made a mental note to sand it and smooth it as best as he could to please Mutti.

As the door swung wide, he stopped abruptly. Something was very wrong.

Darkness. Silence. No appetising smells from the stove, no familiar, welcoming arms.

'Mutti?' he called out, uncertainly, fear gripping him and stopping him in his tracks. But Josef was tougher than it seemed, and within a heartbeat, he was striding down the hallway to the little kitchen, pushing open the door and stopping dead at the sight of his mother. The woman he had known as a tower of strength, the woman who had survived that terrible night and helped him move forward with his life when all he had wanted to do was curl up and weep for his loss. That resilient woman who had loved him unconditionally and never given in to her own grief was sitting, tears rolling down her ashen face, unable to speak past the sobs shaking her thin frame.

His call-up papers were open on the table.

He was called up to join the Army of the Third Reich, to proudly join its ranks the following week, four short days after finishing his exams, and just two days after turning eighteen years old.

No university. No dreams, and worst of all, being wrenched from his childhood home which he had barely managed to reconcile as home anyway since Hans had been taken from them.

His mother, so strong in the bitter aftermath of her first loss, was incoherent with grief and utterly inconsolable now. Day ran into night as they sat and talked, Frieda railing against his fate, clutching at him desperately until he felt compelled to take her hands gently in his, look her in the eyes, and tell her that he had to go.

Harder than seeing his father dragged away, much harder than saying goodbye to his dreams, he had to harden his heart to allow himself to walk out of the door, knowing he was leaving his mother utterly bereft. Karl, who had been called up at the same time, was there to meet him, and as he looked back at his mother's eyes dark with grief, he saw her put her hand to her mouth, sick to the stomach as their hands shot up in the obligatory salute.

***

The training camp was much tougher than he expected. Josef had not thought beyond the moment of leaving, and he was ill-prepared for what was to come. He had glibly assumed it would be a little like the Hitler Youth meetings, much shouting, much posturing, and even more saluting.

On the first morning, the young men were roused by a whistle at dawn. Reeling from their beds, they were ordered into a long, low building where they were given uniforms, boots, a rifle and, oddly, Josef thought, a PE kit.

The PE kit was all they seemed to wear for the next four, interminable weeks. They were drilled, ceaselessly and unrelentingly. When not out running, carrying a full pack with the skin chafing from their bleeding feet, they were oiling, cleaning and reassembling their rifles, over and over again until they could do it with their eyes closed.

'You will be the best,' was the daily challenge and war cry, and each night, Josef collapsed into his narrow bunk with all his muscles on fire and quivering with exhaustion.

He grew tougher. He had no choice, failure was not to be contemplated, nor tolerated. Under no uncertain terms, they were told that they would be fit enough to join the regular army at the end of their training and join the front line to claim the rightful lands of the Third Reich. There was no compromise. But each night as he pulled his meagre blanket over his face, it was all he could do not to weep for his mother, mourn his father's absence, and try to withstand the icy grip of dread around his heart at what he may surely be called to do in the name of the Fatherland.

CHAPTER 14

Josef's War: 1940

Josef rolled over onto his stomach and took a proffered cigarette from the soldier lying on the cold earth next to him. Shielding the flare with a cupped hand, he drew the acrid smoke deep into his lungs, feeling his heart race as the nicotine hit his system.

They were pushing themselves hard, racing towards the North Sea. They had marched across Belgium and had been heading south-west with Paris in their sights, but a week ago their orders had changed. The directive now was to get to the coast before the British, to cut them and their paltry little army off and claim Europe for the Fuhrer. They had marched hard and fast, their training paying off as the miles slid past under the tramping of their heavy boots.

Today, a small town lay ahead, and just like all the other shattered towns lying in their wake, they were to take this and claim it as a base. The tanks and trucks could then roll in after them and establish command, taking food and livestock from the locals to feed their insatiable army.

Josef got quietly to his feet, blinked and peered along the sight of his rifle. The order to advance had come almost as the sun rose, and they began to march calmly towards the walls of the old town. As they approached the mediaeval gates, the mayor appeared to meet them. A single man against a tank battalion, and yet Josef saw the flash of bitter defiance in his eyes as he handed over the flag in his hand, followed by tears as the Swastika was raise d moments later over the Mairie in the town square.

Josef was detailed to find accommodation, and within a few moments, he was marching smartly through the doors of an imposing looking house that appeared to be suitable for his commanding officer's rank.

He stopped for a moment, taking in the beauty of the old manor. Paintings hung everywhere, and dusty books lined the walls. Pushing open the door to a large dining room, a sudden movement caught his eye, a door closing at the end of a narrow passageway to his right. Quietly, he drew his Luger and paced carefully down the hall, doing his best to steady and quieten his breathing.

He was painfully aware that he had not broken his fast that day, and a tremor ran through his hands, making the dull gunmetal shimmer in the dim light. He pushed tentatively against the wooden door ahead of him and stepped silently through into the darkened room beyond. They had experienced little resistance so far, so it was with utter shock that he heard the shot ringing out, and Josef dropped to the floor, completely disorientated and panting with fear. He swung his gun wildly, trying desperately to focus on whoever had fired at him, and seeing a movement in the corner he gripped his pistol with both hands and fired.

A body fell. A tiny whimper. Then reeling with horror as he stood over the child at his feet, her eyes fixed on his with a curious mixture of a plea for help and hatred as her blood gushed from the gunshot wound gaping in her stomach, her hands pressed against herself in a vain attempt to stem the flow.

Slipping in the warm pool as he knelt to try to help her, then clutching her to him as her head dropped back and her little body went limp. Became aware, finally, of a keening sound that might have been coming from his own, bloodless lips, harsh voices and harsher hands peeling her from his arms, his instinct to protect her making him lash out frantically until someone, mercifully, hit him and he fell into a blessed unconsciousness.

***

Josef awoke, aware of crisp sheets for the first time since he had left Mutti behind so many moons ago. He lay very still, knowing that something important had happened, and as the pain in his head returned, with it came the memory of what he had done, and he lurched over the low bed he was lying in, retching from the pit of his stomach onto the clean, tiled floor below.

The splattering sound brought running feet and a cold cloth on his forehead, but no relief from the vision in his mind, attacking him viscerally, the thud, the whimper, his knees skidding in the child's blood. Her eyes, dying but raging, fixed on his with her own and that of her forefathers before her.

He shook his head and peered up at the nurse, her eyes running over him professionally, but with a clear lack of empathy.

'You are not wounded, I see,' she announced, abruptly, her nostrils flaring aggressively as she stared him down. 'There is no need for you to stay. I need this bed for real soldiers, not fainting boys.'

Josef stared after her as she turned on her heel and stalked away, then heard a titter beginning, running like a dirty wave down the line of beds occupying the length of the wall in the room in which he had awoken. The titter turned to jeering as he slid off the bed, and as he had no belongings besides the clothes he stood in and the weapons he strapped to his belt, he slipped out of the ward with his eyes down and his heart sinking lower still.

He thought it could get no worse.

As he made to leave the makeshift hospital, a voice hailed his name. With his gut twisting painfully, he turned to face Karl, wearily raising his arm to match the crisp salute he felt before he even saw it begin.

Karl's sneer told Josef that he had heard the derision aimed at his back. He wondered, fleetingly, if Karl knew what he had done, that he had killed a child, but his next words chilled him to the bone.

'It was just a peasant, Josef. A French peasant. Get over it, she got what she had coming.'

***

The next few days passed in a blur. Josef slipped back into the machine that was the army of the Fatherland, his feet marching in time, his arm rendering perfect salutes, his mind an automaton.

They were to cut the British off and destroy every last man. They were to deliver Europe to the Fuhrer.

Josef was numb, unable to feel, unable to sense any emotion nor notice the pain in his feet at the end of each day's marching. He had become the perfect soldier, outwardly, responding to commands precisely and swiftly without dissent nor complaint.

That day, the end was in sight, along with the rear guard of the British Expeditionary Force. They were so close, they could hear English words floating in the sea breeze, could smell the sweat of desperate men readying for one last fight. When he was picked for night patrol that day, Josef accepted with alacrity. Night patrol meant a small number of men, and better still, silence. No jocular camaraderie, no burning patriotism, just silence. Each man alone with his thoughts, darkness and stealth replacing the mindless crunching of the marching boots of daytime.

They were detailed to sweep the perimeter of their own encampment, ensuring that no desperate British soldiers could slip through on a last killing spree. Josef took the outer line, skirting the huge camp and allowing his eyes to become adapted to the utter darkness of the night. Twenty paces separated him from the next man, and he felt the velvet darkness swallow him up, suddenly relieved to feel alone.

Alone and away from the army. Josef stopped. The desire to leave welled painfully up inside him, to get away from the machine, to be his own man again. His heart began to beat hard against his ribs and it was all he could do to control his breathing so as not to be heard. Deserters were shot. Shot and dishonourably discharged, the shame travelling home to their families but without a body to mourn.

Josef's mind began to flicker through images of the last few weeks like a film, jerking from one scene to another. The girl, a pool of blood. The mayor with tears in his eyes handing over a flag. And onwards to a scene he had not yet envisaged, soldiers fighting for their lives, young men forced to fight against the greed and tyranny of his own Fuhrer. Forced to fight, just as he had been, leaving his mother, his plans and his life in tatters.

And when you no longer fear a bullet between your shoulder blades, your path ahead becomes clear. For Josef, wrapped in his vision and cloaked by night, it was just as easy as putting one foot in front of the other to walk away.

***

He awoke as if from the deepest, most peaceful dream. Josef stretched, then stiffened as leaves brushed his face. He had crept under a hedge some miles away, his heart lightening with each step, and had fallen asleep immediately, something which he had been unable to do since that terrible day when he had killed a child.

Child killer. His eyes snapped open as his mind clanged shut, and he sat up quietly to take stock of his position.

It was near dawn, a silvery light gleaming in the east. Josef smiled inwardly, a simple way to orientate himself and a good time to travel.

But travel where? He exhaled slowly. He was wearing full uniform and was carrying a pistol and a water bottle. He had nothing else to sustain or to hide him from the two armies amassing nearby, and he needed to do something about that quickly.

He sat up carefully and squinted into the early light. This was open country and farmland, and somewhat west of his position, he made out a cluster of low buildings, whether a hamlet or a large farm, he was unable to tell at this distance.

He did not want to go west. Everything instinct told him to run east, back to Germany, back to Mutti. Back to a life that no longer existed. He sighed and the sound made him jump. It was time to leave, and, with a sharp intake of breath, he realised suddenly that he would rather be taken by the British than his own army. That he would much, much rather be a Prisoner of War than fighting for a cause he knew he loathed from the bottom of his heart.

He stood and began to walk towards the distant buildings, materialising as a series of small cottages as he got closer. There were no lights at this hour, and he had no idea what to expect as he approached the door of the first building. All he knew was that there would be no more killing in his own, personal war, and as he walked, he unbuckled his belt and slipped his pistol off it.

Unwilling to shame his mother by scaring another woman, he took a deep, steadying breath and knocked respectfully at the door. And when the old lady came out with fear in her eyes, he knelt and placed the gun in her trembling hands and wept along with her.

***

She fed him and clothed him, burnt his uniform with the same hatred on her face as was mirrored in his own. After he had washed in her outhouse, she gave him clothes, simple but practical, the clothes of a farmworker, and he looked at her with questions in his eyes.

'Mon fils,' she answered, quietly, and he bowed his head in shame. Her son, presumably out there, fighting because his country had gone to war in the short breath of a generation since the sun set on the last.

She reached out, then, and put her hand beneath his chin, lifting his head up to look at him steadily, her old eyes meeting his exhausted gaze. To his surprise, she spoke to him in his own language, accented but clear.

'My husband was German. My son has run from here, he refuses to fight because he is torn in half. You must run too, and you must go now, before they find you. And Josef, you must take your gun too. They will not forgive you if they catch you.'

He held her gaze. 'I cannot go back,' he said, slowly. 'I can't fight for the Fuhrer. I am going to try to get taken by the British, they are not far from here now.'

She nodded. 'Go north. You have about half a day's walk ahead of you. It is best you go before it is too late.'

And with her blessing, his gun in his belt, her son's clothes on his back and her food in his belly, he walked out that day to try to hurry his chosen fate to its inevitable conclusion.

Chapter 15

New Beginnings

Monique rolled out from under the hedge she'd spent the night in, brushing the twigs and leaves from her rough clothes as she stood.

She was trapped and she had no idea which way to turn.

The German army was to the south and east of her, the size of it apparent by the sound of their boots, their trucks and their guttural language which drove cold shafts of fear into her heart each time she heard them curse from afar.

Not far enough. She had no idea now how long she'd been travelling; she'd wandered with no true sense of purpose since the day she was unhomed. Like the farmer she was, she'd scavenged berries as she walked, muttering the names in French then English as she came across them, her heart tightening with the memory of her mother and the life she'd left behind. She had knocked on a few doors and had been met with a wary generosity – she'd been given food but no lodging, the light of cold anger in her eyes discouraging even the kindest of souls from inviting her over their threshold.

Her legs shook. She knew she couldn't go much further, but her fear drove her onwards.

Suddenly, she froze. A man climbed over a gate which she'd just seen ahead of her and dropped down into the road before her. He stopped abruptly, as shocked as she was to find another soul out there at dawn, and then said something to her, called out to her in a soft voice, clearly unwilling to attract attention.

Monique had nowhere to run. He stood before her; the army stood behind. Her terror and the lack of food in the past few days suddenly hit her with what felt like a physical blow, and she fought for breath as she raised her eyes mutely towards his. She couldn't fight off another man, and as the sun came up and blinded her, she was unable to read the concern etched upon his face.

The man stood, stock still, certain that she would flee like a rabbit if he so much as moved a muscle. The sun rising behind him shone full on her waxen face, and as a tiny moan slipped from her lips, Monique's legs finally buckled beneath her, and Josef stepped forward and caught her in his arms.

***

When she came around, Monique's eyelids fluttered then widened in alarm at the sight of the stranger leaning back on his elbows in the long grass, surveying her quietly.

'It's all right.' He soothed her in the same tone as she used to use to soothe her cows while she was milking, and she sat up slowly, noting his rough, farm clothing and heavy boots. His accent sounded unfamiliar, but then again, she realised, she'd wandered many miles from her home over the past few days.

Her stomach growled with hunger, suddenly, and the young man twisted up onto his knees, opened a haversack and obligingly, handed her a small package of waxed paper. Her mouth watered as she smelt the ham within, and he smiled in answer to the question in her eyes.

'I ate well last night,' he said, gently. 'You can have all that.'

Monique smiled, gratefully, and did her best to eat the ham without revealing the depths of her loneliness and hunger of the past few days.

The mood had changed in the villages. The doors were now locked, eyes fearful within. The British were running, the Germans were swarming relentlessly after them in a seemingly unstoppable wave. Nobody dared answer the door to a stranger, and Monique couldn't remember the last time she'd eaten anything other than scraps she'd scavenged that had been thrown to the chickens in the yards she'd trudged through.

'Who are you?' he asked eventually, watching her as she licked her fingertips, then wiped her hands clean on the grass beside her.

She looked up and seemed to notice him properly for the first time. Fair hair, lean and tall, around her own age or perhaps younger, but with a sadness to his blue-grey eyes which went far beyond his years, a look which, had Monique only known, was mirrored in hers.

'I'm Monique,' she answered, seeing no need for deception in this strange place, and feeling oddly at ease with the young man before her. 'I ran away,' she added, and stopped abruptly, unable to speak for the sudden surge of pain the memories brought. He nodded.

'I ran away too,' he said, and like her, stopped, unable or unwilling to elaborate.

Monique drew a sharp breath, made a decision.

'I don't know where to go, now,' she said, her voice breaking. 'I was just trying to get away from... just away, and now there are men fighting everywhere. My mother was English and I'm not afraid of them, but I AM afraid that I might get overtaken by the Germans.' Her voice faltered, then, and he saw a darkness cloud her face.

'I'm not afraid of the British, either,' he murmured, unsure what he should tell her. 'And I think, like you, I want to stay ahead of the Germans too. I'm a long way from home and I can't go back.'

Like Monique, his voice tailed off. Then, seeing her looking at him appraisingly, eyes searching his face, he said, honestly, 'I'm running from them too. I want to go to England.'

Monique smiled, and for the first time, he noticed how pretty she was, tiny freckles showing under her dirty, tanned skin.

'Shall we go together, then?' she asked shyly. 'I have no wish to stay here, there is no place for me here now the Germans have come.'

He smiled too.

'I should like that,' he said, slowly. 'Let's head for the sea, the coast is not far away now.'

And with an oddly formal gesture, he stood and helped her to her feet, and together, they turned north towards the sea and England.

Part 4

Dunkirk

Chapter 16

Lost in the Dark: June 1940

They were lost and alone on the night sea.

Elsie squinted into the darkness, salt stinging her eyes as she fought her exhaustion.

They had started so well. A fair wind, their boat had sped along in the wake of the little ships headed for Dunkirk, a name that had been unfamiliar to them both but was now their whole reason for being.

Then the wind had veered, and they had needed to tack, unable to steer as close to the wind as they would have liked as they shipped wave after wave over their bows.

The steam ships motored steadily onwards, and gradually, one by one, disappeared from view. They were alone on the sea, and, for the first time, Elsie felt utterly bereft. Daniel was asleep, tightly curled under the seat amidships, covered by a blanket and none of his features visible.

He had not said goodnight.

She moved her head left and right, scanning the horizon for other boats, for land. Her chin scraped painfully and bled afresh on the salt-wet edge of her coat, tightly buttoned up against the wind and spray.

Elsie stiffened. There was a sound ahead and she strained to hear it, her ears struggling to distinguish the sounds from the rush to the wind and the spray over their bows.

Voices. Voices crying out, voices keening.

Suddenly, Elsie pushed the tiller hard over, the little boat swerving hard to starboard and the sudden movement waking Daniel from his slumber with a start.

'What's happening?' he hissed, instantly alert, and Elsie nodded to port, not loosening her grip on the tiller with both hands for a second. Daniel turned and stared.

The first boat was returning.

Heavily overloaded, men crouching, huddled against one another and holding on tightly to avoid being thrown over the gunwales riding low in the choppy seas. And then, behind this little ship, another and then another, all chugging slowly, all loaded with men on every deck, every surface that could possibly hold the weight of a desperate man.

Elsie and Daniel watched in shocked silence as they began to pass the returning boats, port to straining port.

'We're too late.' Daniel said, eventually, and Elsie turned away from him, tears spilling over. Pulling the main sheet in tighter and feeling the boat heel over a little more as her speed picked up.

Hours later, it seemed, and dawn broke over a choppy sea. They had not seen another boat for some time, but they had lost count of how many had passed them during those terrible hours of darkness. Elsie had stared at each and every craft, scanning the decks for Jack but not seeing her brother. Seeing injuries and blood, men weeping and men vomiting.

'We can't stop,' she replied, steadily. 'Jack might be there, still. They can't have taken them all, surely? It was an army.'

The last words were torn from her throat in a tight little wail, and Daniel reached over and hugged her, blinking hard.

'We carry on.' he said, firmly. 'We've come this far, we have to see it for ourselves now.'

Elsie smiled at him, gratefully, relief flooding through her cold chest and warming her heart.

Deep inside, she'd known Daniel would never let her down.

***

Monique and Josef crouched behind the hedgerow, holding their breath. The German soldiers marching past on the other side had seemed to come from nowhere, and they had pushed through the undergrowth and flattened themselves, desperate to avoid being caught at this stage.

'Hawthorn, *aubépine*,' Monique muttered under her breath. 'Holly, *houx*,' the litany of her mother and her childhood sending a wave of calm through her even as her hands bled from the thorns.

Josef stood, eventually, and reached down to help her up from the ditch into which they had scrambled.

'We are so close,' he said. 'And they are gone now.' He looked at her, appraisingly. 'Your English is excellent. I wish mine was as good, but my accent is not, shall we say, authentic.'

He laughed, and Monique answered, 'I can't actually place you. Your accent is so different to where I come from.'

Josef frowned.

'I come from a long way east, close to the border with Germany.' He bit his lip, then, knowing that he was telling her half-truths.

He couldn't bring himself to tell her which side of the border.

They walked on, more cautiously now, sticking to the field side of the hedgerow until dusk began to fall. Soon, the visibility became too difficult to continue on the rough ground, and they climbed through the hedge at the first opportunity. Both felt the change as the salt breeze caught their nostrils.

A sea change indeed. The lane they had been following was beginning to peter out. As it began to rise up a brow, they began to increase their pace as the breeze freshened. Approaching the crest, they saw the sea ahead of them, and both stopped and stared at the beach rolling down towards the sea, moonlight catching the breakers as they swept into the shore.

Monique looked at Josef, and without thinking, she reached out and caught his hand. Suddenly, they were running, running like children to the sand, their destination beckoning and the excitement coursing through them. Monique threw her head back and laughed, and Josef laughed too, the first carefree sound they had made since they had met.

The gunfire came from nowhere.

Nowhere and everywhere, the sound pinning Monique to the ground, sand in her eyes and nose and mouth, choking with it and paralysed by fear. Josef lay across her, utterly still, his weight pressing her deeper into the sand so she panicked suddenly and twisted her head violently to the side so she could take a deep, clear breath. As she did, she felt his hand press against her lips, stopping her from crying out, but letting her know that he was not a dead weight, he was alive.

She whimpered against his hand; the tiny sound lost in the terrible noise still reverberating around them.

The gunfire was coming from just around the headland to their right as they faced the sea. Waves and waves of it but beginning to lessen as the interminable moments crept on.

Monique had no idea how long they lay there, but the sky had darkened to inky black by the time the firing stopped, and Josef loosened his grip on her prostrate body.

'Follow me,' he whispered, urgently, his breath warm against her ear, and, taking her hand, he pulled her up into a crouching run towards the dunes they had run over earlier in their childish excitement. Monique ran silently, her breath seeming to rasp in her ears and her legs on fire with cramp at running after staying still for so long.

She collapsed into the sea grass and rolled onto her back, clutching her knees to her chest and trying to calm her breathing.

Josef did the same, then recovering fast, he crawled to a gap between the little dunes and the scant cover they afforded.

'They're leaving,' he whispered, amazement in his voice,' they're all going.'

Monique rolled again and crawled to where he was lying stretched flat on the cold sand.

She could scarcely believe what she was seeing.

Lines of men stretching out into the sea. Bullets whining overhead still, fewer than earlier now that darkness had fallen, but all the more frightening for the sudden sound cutting through the night sky.

And boats. Boats as far as she could see, men scrambling aboard and each little craft turning her nose to the sea as soon as she was full to the gunwales. Men clutching at each boat as she left, then surging towards the next in a desperate hope that this might be the one to take them away from the hell unfolding on the beach.

'Is it all over?' she said. 'Have the Germans won?'

Josef found her hand and squeezed it tightly.

'I don't know,' he muttered, 'but I'm not going to stay around to find out. Will you come?'

Monique stared. 'Yes,' she answered, finally, 'but how do we do it? We can't just walk into the sea.'

Josef took a deep breath and met her eyes. 'I think that's exactly what we have to do.'

***

Elsie began to struggle with the tiller. She had her eye firmly on the line of breakers marking a sandbank, and she was doing her utmost to work her way towards it and the last few soldiers waiting for their turn.

The problem was, other boats were beating her to it, the low chug of their engines alerting her to their proximity in the shifting light. The wind had altered in the past hour, and she and Daniel were exhausted, beating up into it, waves breaking over their bows and soaking them again and again, the salt chafing their faces raw now.

She was nearly spent. Daniel lay in the bottom of the boat out of the wind. The pain from his leg and the cold had taken their toll. His face was ashen, and his eyes were closed. Elsie had been at the helm for hours now, and since the wind had swung around, she'd had to work harder and harder to hold their course.

She wished, suddenly and fervently, that they had an engine. She wished her father was alive. More than anything, she wished she wasn't at the helm of this folly of her own making.

Another boat cut across them suddenly, close enough for her to swing the tiller and head downwind to give them both sea room. The relief was instant and enormous. The little boat lifted and surfed as she let the sail out, riding before the wind so the incessant waves over the bow ceased and the chill wind in their faces disappeared as they ran with the wind, instead of beating into it.

Daniel stirred with the altered motion and looked up at her, his eyes dull with fatigue. Elsie immediately swung the tiller again to regain their course, and then sobbed aloud as the strain of holding the tiller hard against the wind threatened to beat her.

'Let it go, Elsie.'

She opened the eyes which she'd squeezed shut against the tears and the waves, saw his face close to hers, his eyes full of guilt for her exhaustion and knowing he couldn't help her.

'Let it go,' he repeated, then reached out and pulled the tiller so that the boat swung again, away from the wind and from the sandbank lined with the last few soldiers waiting, always waiting and clutching as their chances came and went.

'I can't leave them' – she wept – 'what if Jack's still there?'

Daniel swung away from her, staring at the elusive bank. Cupping his hands to his mouth, he yelled at the top of his voice.

'Jack. Jack Derham. Jack!'

No answer came, just a collective sigh of exhausted men, eyes turning from the little sailing boat and out to sea, to the next boat heading towards them and the chance of rescue.

'He's not there,' he said, unnecessarily.

Elsie bit her lip and winced as she tasted blood.

And then she saw them.

Not a hundred yards away and downwind in the path of the boat, two figures were stumbling into the water, waves swirling around their waists as they pushed deeper, calling with an urgency borne of desperation.

'That way,' she snapped, and Daniel turned his gaze to where she was pointing, in the next moment leaning out amidships at the boat's lowest reach from the water and extending his arms towards the pair.

As Daniel reached for the first pair of hands, he seemed to hesitate for a second, then heaved as the figure scrambled up and fell, panting into the bottom of the boat. Then he turned to the next person, taller than the first and already trying to haul himself up over the wide wooden gunwale unaided. As he lurched upwards, he seemed to stagger. His foot caught, and Daniel grasped his hand firmly.

'Elsie,' he gasped as the man seemed to fall back. 'Elsie, help me.'

But Elsie was already alongside him, reaching down into the dark water to try to free his foot which was snarled up on something she couldn't see, a branch, perhaps? Not a branch. Her hands encountered what felt like coarse material, and she hauled it up as hard as she could to free the man's boot.

The scream was like a wounded animal. The man's foot came free, and Elsie stared at the flaccid features of the drowned soldier whose gear had ensnared him as she screamed and screamed again. Daniel whirled towards her as Elsie turned blindly towards him, the dead man spinning down into the depths as she let go of his greatcoat.

The sudden silence was deafening.

Then Elsie gave a gasping sob, and Daniel held her face against him, muffling the stricken sounds into his chest.

Seconds later, the keel struck sand, and without a word, Elsie pulled away and grabbed the tiller which was swinging untended, and Daniel reached to haul the flapping main sheet. The boat answered the wind and pulled gamely away from the beach, her keel scraping but not sticking as they swung her nose around away from the horrors they had seen, back towards the open Channel and home.

CHAPTER 17

All at Sea

Daybreak came, and as the pale light caught their young faces, the four stared at each other, taking stock.

To Elsie's amazement, she found herself looking at a girl perhaps a few years older than herself, long light brown hair bundled back from her exhausted face. Tentatively, Elsie smiled, and the girl smiled back, shyly holding out her hand and offering her name.

'Monique,' repeated Elsie, 'but why were you in the sea?'

'We were both running for the same reason,' interjected the blond man, his long legs scrunched up uncomfortably beneath him on the deck. 'We both had to get away from the Germans. They've overrun our homes and we have nowhere to go now.' His voice caught, and he broke her gaze, staring over the bow.

'They took my farm,' added Monique, and tears swelled in her throat.

Elsie dropped her eyes, seeing that Monique was close to breaking down. Turning to Daniel, she asked, 'Where shall we head back to? What's our best course?'

He shrugged.

'We go with the wind. We've been heading north during the night, but it's turning easterly now, so if we head west, it'll be more comfortable, and I suppose we have no need to go back to Ramsgate.'

The last words held a question, and Elsie shook her head, decisively.

'No need,' she agreed. 'Let's get as far west as we can, and just land for the night. We need food and a proper dry place to sleep.' She shivered suddenly. 'Then I want to get home as soon as we can. Back home to Christchurch.'

She looked round and saw Monique and Josef watching them, mutely.

'Get some sleep,' she said kindly. 'You'll have to share the tarpaulin. We normally take it in turns, but I reckon you can both get under together if you don't mind?'

Josef smiled at Monique, who, to her horror, blushed to the roots of her hair. 'We've slept in some strange places lately.' He grinned, and suddenly, all four of them were smiling broadly.

Daniel helped shake out the tarpaulin, and within a few moments, Josef and Monique were curled up, back-to-back and fast asleep, lulled by the steady rocking of the boat.

Daniel looked at Elsie and saw the fatigue written all over her drawn features.

'I'll take the helm now. You've been on it for hours,' he said.

Elsie threw him such a look of gratitude that his heart ached. He threw his blanket, Elsie catching it deftly and hunkering down into as comfortable a position as she could find with the extra passengers on-board.

Within minutes, she too was asleep, and Daniel swung the bow towards the west, let out the mainsheet and began to run with the wind.

***

The dream came again, clawing him from his peaceful sleep back into the world of nightmares.

He was lying on his side, his face against the cold floor, watching a slick of blood seeping ever closer. The girl was kneeling, her hands pressed against her side, blood pouring between her fingers and gushing onto the flagstones, the metallic smell assailing his nostrils and making his stomach churn with rising nausea.

He wanted to help her, but each time he reached out towards her, she knocked his hands away with one of her own, more blood escaping each time she let go of her wound. Helping her was making it worse, but he couldn't seem to stop himself, and soon she was lying next to him, too weak to kneel, her unforgiving eyes fixed upon his own ashamed gaze. He tried to raise his head, but something was holding him back, and suddenly the crimson tide reached him, warm blood washing against his face and into his mouth, choking his cries for help.

Josef came awake. Rolling over onto his hands and knees, he wiped his mouth with the back of his shaking hand, the taste of the blood still fresh from the dream.

Aware suddenly of complete silence, he looked up in confusion.

Daniel and Elsie were staring at him, shock etched on their faces. But Monique – oh Monique – the look on her face was vying between fury and revulsion.

'You were sleep talking,' she whispered. 'In German. You were sleep talking in German.'

Josef felt his stomach contract with horror and swallowed hard, his eyes fixed on hers.

'Are you German?' she insisted, and when he gave the smallest of nods, she turned and spat over the side.

'Monique.' he faltered, then rallied. 'Monique, you know me. I would never hurt you. I am not one of them.'

Monique threw him a look of utter contempt, then turned her back as best as she could in the deck space she had, fixing her eyes on the horizon and cutting him out of her sight.

Daniel and Elsie carried on staring at Josef. Neither of them had ever seen a real German, and this man did not fit what they had come to expect.

Josef was dressed in the rough clothes of a French farmer and was not bristling with weaponry. More to the point, he had given Monique more than her share of the tarp and blanket during the night, details which both Daniel and Elsie had noted, assuming that they were lovers, or at least, very close. He had unwrapped a package of ham and cheese at daybreak and broken it up into four portions, sharing easily as if hunger was not gnawing cruelly at his insides.

But Monique's reaction was visceral and hard to ignore.

Daniel cleared his throat and spoke first.

'We thought you were French,' he began. 'We thought you were running from the Germans. Why would you run if you're one of them?'

Josef flinched.

'I may be German by birth,' he replied, 'but I am NOT one of them. The Nazis took my father away for no reason. They sent me to war when I was supposed to be going to university, and I had to leave my mother all alone…' His voice broke.

Daniel looked away, embarrassed, giving him time to compose himself.

Josef continued, 'I met Monique a few days ago. She was running because they took her farm. I was running because I cannot fight this war for them, I will not kill innocent people for no reason.'

Elsie broke in. 'Daniel, couldn't we hide him?'

Josef shook his head wearily. 'I don't need to hide. I want to be taken. If I am a Prisoner of War in your country, I am safe and don't need to fight for the Fuhrer. Just hand me in to the police when we get ashore.'

Elsie stared. 'You'd rather go to prison than go home?'

Josef gave a bitter laugh.

'I would much rather it was that way, yes,' he replied, and turned a hopeful face towards Monique. 'I refuse to fight for them. I am not one of them,' he repeated, but when she refused to acknowledge him, he turned his own face away to hide the bitter tears which he could no longer restrain from falling.

***

They made landfall at dusk, after guiding the little boat on a tortuous route to shore through the vicious spikes of the sea defences that stretched as far as they could see in each direction, and while there was clearly the remains of a busy market from earlier in the day, there were few people around and they never did discover which little quay they had pulled in alongside. All the street signs were gone now, in the vain hope of confusing the enemy in the event of an invasion, and the anonymous little town had little to distinguish itself.

Josef roused himself on arrival and swiftly made himself useful with one of Daniels' fishing rods.

'I used to go fishing with my father before the war started,' he answered Elsie's questioning look. 'Never at sea, though, always in our local river, but it can't be too different.'

He must have been right, because by the time Daniel and Elsie had moored up safely for the night, and Monique had busied herself clearing space for the four of them to sleep on the little deck, he had caught two sizeable fish, which he promptly gutted and cleaned in a bucket he borrowed from Daniel.

They lit a fire with driftwood, taking care to cover the flare in the blackout with the tarpaulin they usually slept under. The smoke drove three of them out, with Monique left grimly prodding their supper alone.

She had not said a single word since the morning.

Josef looked at Daniel and Elsie, who shrugged helplessly.

'I think we should pair up tonight,' she said. 'You and Daniel together, and me and Monique.'

'It would, perhaps, be easier,' agreed Josef, although a tiny knife twisted in his heart as he concurred.

They ate the char-grilled fish with their fingers, hunger stopping any conversation or formality. Daniel smiled sadly at Elsie as they prepared to slip into their unfamiliar sleeping areas. Monique and Elsie snuggled up under the bow, with Josef and Daniel in the more exposed stern.

Three of them fell asleep almost immediately, but Josef stayed awake, his eyes staring up at the stars as he blinked back more tears. His heart ached for his mother. She'd already lost her husband. Was she now to lose all contact with her son too, for the rest of the war? And what would it mean if Germany won – would they all be reunited, a proper family again? And what about if the Allies won? Would they execute him?

He rolled over, missing the feeling of Monique's back against his own, as it had been over the past few nights before she discovered who he really was, or who she *thought* he really was. He corrected his own thoughts, angrily. He rolled again, trying not to think about where his father might be, what he might be suffering, or even if he were still alive at all. Thoughts like this took his mind away, and he couldn't afford to lose his wits in this new and possibly vengeful country.

It took until dawn before he fell into an uneasy sleep.

***

Elsie awoke and climbed out from under the tarp quietly so as not to awaken Monique. Glancing at the stern, she saw that Daniel was waking, and she motioned silently for him to join her as she slipped ashore.

They walked for a time in silence. Then, looking fixedly ahead, Elsie asked, 'Do you think he'll be safe if we turn him in?'

Daniel sighed. 'I have no idea,' he answered honestly. 'But I think we have to, Elsie. In fact, he wants us to, and surely that's the best thing?'

She thought for a moment. 'Where do we take him, then?'

'The police station in Christchurch, and I think we should do it as soon as we get home, or we might get into trouble for harbouring him.'

Elsie looked at him, doubtfully. 'They know us though. Surely, they wouldn't suspect us of anything? We were only trying to help rescue Jack.' Her voice broke.

'There's a war on,' Daniel replied, brutally. 'We have to turn him in, Elsie, or we could get arrested for harbouring the enemy.'

The sadness on her face broke his heart, and he made to move towards her, but his crutch caught on a root and as he staggered to catch his balance, Elsie moved out of reach, avoiding contact with him in a way she'd never done before.

'I imagine he is about the same age as Jack,' she said, carefully. 'We don't know his story, Daniel. He might not have wanted to fight at all.'

Daniel stopped and stared at her. 'It makes no difference,' he replied. He's German and there's an end to it.'

Elsie returned his stare, seeing his beloved features cold as stone. Her best friend couldn't see what she could see – just another boy caught up in someone else's war. Just another boy without his family, miles from home, and no idea when or if he would ever see it again.

She turned on her heel and deliberately stalked away too fast for her crippled companion to reach her.

***

They sailed as soon as the tide turned in their favour, familiar landmarks appearing as they entered the choppy waters of the Solent. Daniel passed the tiller to Elsie as they rounded Hurst, the ancient castle lurking darkly as the little boat hugged the channel close to the shore. He joined Monique in the bow, both of them hunkering down and shutting their eyes against the spray that the lively breeze was flinging in their faces.

Elsie would normally have loved the exhilaration of this point of sail, the boat heeling tightly as they thrashed their passage close to the wind, the bow ploughing her path through the head on waves.

But Josef's misery was written across his face, and she couldn't bear to see his plight.

'Talk to me,' she whispered, suddenly, and Josef started at her voice. 'Talk to me. Who are you? Where do you come from, and how did you get into this mess?'

Josef smiled, but it did not touch the bitterness in his eyes.

'Thank you for asking, but what can I say? I'm German, yes, but my family are not Nazis. We are a liberal family, my father was...' He faltered... '*Is* a teacher, a professor of history and he tried to warn people what would happen if we laid down and took what they are forcing us to do.'

Over the next few hours, he told her his story as the waves crashed against the hull. Told her about the day his father was taken and about the day he found he would have to leave his mother alone. About the food shortages that he had grown up with, which made him fear now for her health. About the Nazi Youth and the end of his university dreams. And while he told her about the day he deserted the army of the Third Reich, he faltered again over his words, and although he didn't lie, he left out what had happened at the chateau. The girl's eyes taunted him as he failed to speak of her death, and he knew in his mind that he would never be free of what he had done.

Elsie watched him talking, his blond hair falling over his eyes as he bowed his head to hide his shame, and with an intuitive leap, knew that he had missed something out, something which he couldn't bear to tell her. She watched the tears run between his fingers as he covered his eyes and wept, finally, and she reached out to touch him.

'I'm so sorry about your father,' she murmured, and was rewarded by Josef's hand reaching out suddenly and squeezing hers. She returned the pressure, the first human touch she'd felt since the new distance between her and Daniel and was comforted by his warmth. He looked up finally, caught her looking at him, and smiled tiredly.

And as she returned his gaze, she saw Daniel's face, beyond Josef's, his eyes fixed on their clasped hands and his mouth twisted in a tight grimace, and to her immeasurable shame, she dropped Josef's hand as if she'd been burnt, and turned her face back into the wind.

***

They negotiated the sea defences once again, slowly working their way through and then anchoring near the steep banks of the Run at Mudeford to wait for the tide to turn fully in their favour. Both Daniel and Elsie knew this was necessary and acted without speaking, Monique and Josef watching respectfully and understanding the reason as they saw the troubled waters of the Run back into the harbour.

When the turbulence began to settle, Daniel hauled up the anchor and Elsie took the tiller once again, guiding the boat with casual skill up the narrow channel between the steep banks and into the wider harbour beyond. Her eyes picked out the ugly stakes spiking through the sand that she'd played on since childhood, shuddering at the thought of the mines beneath them. Then she heard Josef's breath catch as the ancient Priory swung into view, the evening sunlight catching the old stone so that it glowed in the distance.

'Beautiful,' Josef whispered, and was rewarded by a smile from Elsie and a scowl from Daniel. Like Monique, he seemed to have decided to cut Josef out of the equation, ignoring him as surely as if it had just been the three of them in the boat.

Monique also gazed at the old church, tears blurring her eyes as homesickness hit her.

'Church, *l'eglise*,' she murmured.

The little church in her village with the flowers in the hedgerow seemed suddenly a lifetime ago and an insurmountable distance and her heart ached with the memory of her mother's gravestone, which must surely be covered in weeds now that her daughter was too far away to tend it.

She started suddenly at the touch of Elsie's hand. She had seen the tears and her natural instinct was to reach out and comfort her, although Monique had withdrawn from them all so much in the past few days that her touch was tentative, expecting a rebuttal. But her need for comfort was all-consuming, and Monique returned the squeeze fiercely, her tears spilling over as she gazed towards the little town ahead, unable to look at Elsie for fear of breaking down completely.

'The tide is just right for the mooring,' she said quietly, and Daniel nodded as she swung the tiller towards the creek by Fisherman's Bank, the place where they had first met so long ago and in such an uncomplicated time compared to this war-torn summer.

They moored up to the buoy and, for the first time in days, Daniel smiled at Elsie as she slid over the side. Her toes found purchase in the silt, and she grinned at the others.

'It's now or never,' she said. 'The tide is rising, and we can carry our stuff ashore now… or wait for it to drop again and get muddier.'

The lightness of her tone belied the tension in her heart, a tension borne from the certain knowledge that she was about to lose Josef to the authorities, and it felt utterly wrong to her. Wrong to turn in a young person simply trying to live his life, look after his mother and do the right thing. A person whom she knew could have, should have been a friend, but for his Aryan blood.

She yanked at the wooden edge of the boat and snapped abruptly, 'I said, it's now or never.' And dropped her eyes in shame as she saw Josef standing quietly with his battered backpack, seeing that he had made himself ready for this moment in a way a man might ready himself for the gallows.

Chapter 18

Home Coming

The sound of the child crying stopped Elsie in her tracks, even as she registered the glow of light shining through the kitchen door. Daniel careered into her as she stopped dead and then pulled himself up as it dawned on him what he was hearing.

'She wouldn't…' he whispered.

'She just bloody did.' Elsie swore and pushed the door so hard it swung open with a bang.

Sudden silence ensued.

Elsie stood and glared at the shocked faces before her, her mother clutching Daisy to her shoulder, another person wheeling around from where he was tending the stove on his knees.

It was Jack.

'Jack?' she whispered, disbelieving her own eyes, and he stood, staring at her and then at the people behind her.

'Where on Earth have you been?' he asked.

Elsie laughed bitterly. 'To Dunkirk, Jack. To try to find you while you were here playing happy families in our house.'

A look of complete confusion passed over Jack's face as he looked from her to Daniel, taking in their dirty, salt-stained clothing.

'Dunkirk?' He faltered.

Daniel nodded firmly. 'We came to try to find you, to try to help. We sailed as soon as we heard the news, but we were too slow. But we did save some people…'

Now it was Daniel's turn to falter.

Jack looked past him to Monique and Josef, his face full of questions, and unable to bear it any longer, Josef stepped forwards and dropped his pack to the ground. In the most perfect English accent Elsie had ever heard him muster, he looked Jack straight in the eye.

'Your sister saved us. We were both running from the Germans. Monique lost her farm…'

He looked round as Monique let out a tiny sob and he reached out to her, and for the first time in days, allowed him to take her hand, gave him an infinitesimal nod of support.

'…and I, I am German. But I am a deserter and refuse to fight in their army, so now I need to turn myself in to you.'

And as an appalled silence descended upon the warm glow of the family kitchen, he pulled his service revolver out of his belt, knelt, and presented it, handle first and with utter formality, to the man who stood over him.

Monique was the first to speak.

'Well, take it then,' she snapped, and Jack seemed to visibly come to his senses and reached out to take the proffered pistol, holding it as if it were burning his hand. He looked back to Elsie, helpless questions crowding his face.

'Let's all sit down,' she ordered gruffly. 'We've been sailing for days, and we are cold and hungry. All of us.' she snapped, seeing the reticence in Jack's demeanour.

She turned then, looked her mother directly in the eye.

'You didn't waste much time. What did you do, get on the first train as soon as I'd walked out of the door? Hoping to beat me back, were you?'

Betsy dropped her eyes, burying her face in her youngest daughter's warm little neck. She took a deep breath, then said,

'I know you don't believe me, Elsie, love. I know you think it is all about the house, and yes, if I'm honest, I was desperate to find somewhere for me and Daisy after Jim left. But Elsie, Jack, I want so much to try to start afresh with you.'

She burst into tears then, and as Daisy stirred, she held out the little girl towards Elsie, who took her and tenderly held her cheek to cheek. Daisy snuffled against her skin and settled immediately, Elsie feeling a glow of something she hadn't felt in a long time, both love and need all in one tiny body.

She looked at Jack.

'We do need to rest,' she said, firmly.' Josef knows he needs to be turned in, but it doesn't need to be right now. If you have enough food here for a simple meal now, it can be in the morning after we've all eaten and had some sleep.'

And so it came to pass that a German deserter, a British soldier, a French refugee, a cripple, a mother and two half-sisters came to rest under one roof while the countries of the world hurled its weapons at one another deep into that dark and restless night.

***

Morning came, and with it, a reckoning.

Elsie woke at first light, lay there listening to the seagulls on the roof until her senses finally told her that she'd come home.

Rolling out of the bed where she had slept end to end with Monique, her toes curled as they touched the cold wooden floor, and she reached for her old slippers, miraculously under the bed from what seemed like a lifetime ago.

Slipping stealthily down to the kitchen, she knelt before the old stove and stoked it up to a fine blaze, filling the kettle and putting it on the top for the brew she was craving.

She knew Jack was there before she turned around, greeting him with a tremulous smile.

'Did you really sail to Dunkirk?' he asked, and when she nodded, his face filled with awe. 'That was some feat.'

'I just wanted to help. We were there in Ramsgate, and we saw all the other boats and heard the news. I just wanted to try to find you.'

Tears welled in her eyes and Jack stepped forwards to enclose her in a rough hug. 'What the hell were you doing in Ramsgate anyway?'

'Trying to find Mum.' She looked down, then said, 'did you get my letter? About Dad?'

Jack hugged her harder. 'Yes, I did. I'm so thankful that you wrote to me rather than getting home to find it out.'

He paused. 'It was so strange, arriving back. I came by train and walked from the station, and it seemed like nothing had changed since we were children, except for the blackout. It took me ages to get here, then when I opened the door, Mum was sitting in the rocking chair with little Daisy, and for a minute I remembered her holding you just like that, in the very same place.'

His words choked up in his throat and he stopped, Elsie returning the hug.

'It's been such a long time since we were a proper family,' she said. 'It's good to have you back, Jack. And' – her face softening – 'isn't our little sister beautiful?'

Jack smiled. 'She is, indeed,' he agreed. 'A bit of a surprise, but so sweet.'

Their moment musing upon their new sister was broken abruptly. They both jumped at the sound of boots on the threshold and looked around as Josef walked through the back door, a chill draught following his footsteps.

He was fully clothed but looked like he'd spent time in the sea. His hair was wet, and his face appeared to be scoured and scrubbed, his skin tight across his high cheekbones and his mouth taut.

Elsie took a breath, but before she could speak, Josef held up his hand.

'I am putting you all at risk,' he said quietly. 'I cannot stay a moment longer. Anyone could have seen the boat coming in last night, someone could be counting heads.'

He looked briefly at Jack, then long and hard at Elsie.

'You know I have to go now,' he said, and to her shock, Elsie felt a whimper swelling in her chest, swallowed hard to stop an inexcusable outburst which she would struggle to justify to herself, let alone her soldier brother.

'I'll go with you,' she managed, weakly, then turned as another voice cut harshly into the cold early light of the little kitchen.

'No. I'll go,' said Daniel, leaning on his crutch but standing taller than she could remember seeing for some time.

His eyes were hard and not open to negotiation. Elsie shivered. This was not the Daniel she knew, the boy she'd poured her heart out to, the boy who had saved her and whom she had saved in her turn.

In a moment of clarity, she saw the depths of his jealousy. She remembered the twist of his face when he saw her comforting Josef. She saw his crutch against Josef's stature, realised that the jealousy was not just directed at her, it was directed at Josef and against a much higher deity – that the anger and bitterness that, until now, he had borne which such dignity, was finally unleashed against an acceptable enemy.

Josef did not stand a chance.

He looked at Elsie and swung his kitbag up onto his shoulder, grimacing as the strap met his salt-chafed skin.

'Thank you,' he said simply. 'Thank you for coming when you did. You saved us both.'

Elsie's eyes filled with tears as Josef turned to go.

'Wait,' she said, and rushed back upstairs, casting around desperately for something to give him, something to help him through the rest of his war.

She could see nothing. Nothing of any value that could possibly impart upon him how much she'd begun to care for him in these past few days at sea. But as she turned to the stairs, her eyes lit upon her childhood shell collection arrayed on the dusty windowsill, and she took her favourite shell, the one which held the music of the sea when she'd held it to her ear in her childhood and pushed it into her pocket.

Dropping her head, she walked back down into the kitchen and cut him a hunk of bread and carved a couple of slices of ham from the pantry. Wrapping it all in paper with the shell concealed inside the packet, she thrust it out to him, not trusting herself to speak, and within the blink of an eye, the thoughtful, introspective young man that had made such a deep impression upon her was gone.

Jack looked and saw her stricken face, but as Monique entered the room then, he thought better than to remark upon it.

***

Life fell into a strange little routine over the next few days.

Daniel was out on his boat from dawn until dusk, scrubbing decks, oiling woodwork and mending rents in the sails.

Nobody commented on the fact that he had not left to go back to his home. Elsie knew that he couldn't face going back to an empty hearth after these weeks of companionship, and he and Jack seemed perfectly happy sharing the little back bedroom between them.

She and Monique were sharing her room, and Mum and little Daisy were in what had been Dad's room, and Elsie shook herself remembering what had been their marital bed.

It was such a long time ago, and so much of her memory was blurred by bitterness and grief. But even through this, she realised that she was coming to love having little Daisy around, and that the silence she and her mother shared was now, more often than not, companionable.

The inevitable happened after this calm interlude, which they all silently acknowledged had to end.

Jack's papers came, and a letter asking for any able-bodied women of the house to come and register for war work.

And when Daniel saw both missives, he took his boat out for the passage of two tides, and returned to his own home, empty-handed and sick at heart.

Part 5

Land Girls

Chapter 19

PoWs: 1944

Elsie rolled over on her hard pallet and blinked sleep out of her eyes. Sun was beginning to filter through the dust motes in the air of the stuffy little attic bedroom which she'd shared for the past four years with Monique.

They had taken so easily to life as land girls. Monique had run her farm almost single-handedly for most of her young years, and while Elsie preferred fishing, she discovered a simple pleasure in planting seeds, hoeing weeds, and harvesting the fruits of their labours.

She had wanted to stay with Daniel for her war work. She knew he would struggle to fish alone (his injuries were a lifelong reminder of the tough life he had chosen) and that they had always worked well as a team.

But Daniel utterly withdrew from her after he took Josef to the police station, withdrew in body and soul. He moved back into his own home, leaving a hole in her life just as turmoil was unleashed again by the call to arms, and while she understood his reasons, in her heart she struggled to forgive him for leaving without a backwards glance.

He never told her what happened or where Josef was to be taken. Monique never asked, and his name was never spoken again under their roof. Only Elsie seemed to feel the lack of him, the steadfast look in his eyes as he scanned the horizon, his calm voice describing his origins. Origins based in family, in love and in peace.

Rolling over in bed that morning, four long years later, she thought of him as always and sent him a little prayer, knowing that, for anyone ready to listen, Josef was not, and never had been, their enemy.

There had been much activity around their farm of recent weeks, farm machinery rolling down their little lane and out onto the cropped grass of the New Forest heath, disappearing from view behind the unruly rows of gorse and displacing puzzled looking ponies as they did so.

Nobody seemed to know what was going on until the day they saw the first lorries passing along the freshly gravelled track. Lorries with aeroplane parts stowed under tarpaulin; lorries carrying building supplies; lorries carrying men with baggy brown trousers and faded shirts.

'Prisoners of war,' pronounced Monique, and spat on the ground.

Elsie turned and stared at her. 'How do you know?'

'I just know. Every last one of them a Bosch.'

Monique had grown harder over the past few years, her hatred of the Germans increasing week by week, month by month. Elsie had asked her what had happened to her at the farm, but Monique never answered beyond a simple Gallic shrug and a dismissive 'they came. They took what they saw. They took everything they wanted, so I left.'

Elsie turned back and looked at the men jumping down from the lorries. They were all thin, she saw, but appeared strong and able, each one reaching into the open backed trucks to unload tools, shovels, pickaxes and more.

As they swung their loads up onto their shoulders, each turned and squinted into the sun before falling into line, the look of resignation on their faces one and the same. Clearly, each was used to hard labour and was expecting nothing less, and as they began to march into the sunrise, Elsie guessed they were unlikely to be able to appreciate the breathtaking beauty of the Forest as the sun caught the gleam of yellow on the gorse and the purple of the heather.

Each man the same, each man loaded down by his pack and even more so by his memories.

But Elsie bit her lip hard so that Monique would never know that these were not faceless prisoners, that each man was not the same. That some of the memories were shared.

That as one man straightened his shoulders and began to march, he caught her eye and deliberately returned her stare.

Thinner. Older and tired, but unmistakably Josef.

***

Information filtered through slowly, in the form of gossip and tittle tattle. While everyone was always told to 'keep mum,' the news gradually leaked that the PoWs were detailed to build a runway, one of a whole series being constructed in the New Forest, ready for the long-hoped for invasion.

But Elsie sought other news, and one day, she discovered the knowledge she craved.

She overheard a conversation between two drivers in the scullery of the large farmhouse where she and Monique were based. Both were young women, trained to drive trucks since the beginning of the war, and deeply absorbed in their conversation in the way that lonely women may be. Neither noticed Elsie standing quietly in the doorway.

'Where are you headed now?' asked the taller of the two.

'Back to pick up more equipment. How about you?'

'I'm knocking off for the day, after I've dropped the men on the first work shift back to Ossemsley.'

Elsie took a silent step backwards, then tiptoed out of the hall before she let her breath go in a rush. Ossemsley was just to the south, a bare four miles away and an easy hike for a woman on a mission.

She spent the day in an agony of suspense. Twice, Monique snapped at her because she was slow to catch the hay she was throwing down from the back of the cart. Once more, she daydreamed and failed to notice when she was told to lead the cart horses back to the barn for the evening, earning her a tongue lashing from the farmer's wife, Mrs Pidgley, and a puzzled glance from Monique as her eyes filled with nervous tears.

'What's the matter?' she whispered as they sat at the scrubbed pine table in the kitchen after tea, but Elsie just shook her head.

'Time of the month,' she muttered, and Monique squeezed her hand sympathetically.

But when they went up to bed that night, Monique lay staring at the ceiling until she fell asleep, wondering why her friend of four years had lied to her. All the girls on the farm, living in close proximity now for so long, had the same cycle, and she knew that Elsie was not due.

Elsie waited until she heard Monique's breathing become calm and regular before she rose silently. She had slipped her trousers and jumper under her blanket as she went to bed, and stealthily wriggled into them, hardly daring to breathe. She padded out of their little attic room in her stockinged feet and slipped on her boots, which all the girls left by the back step.

She was relieved to see a full moon, as she had no torch and wouldn't have dared to break the blackout even if she had.

Taking a moment to orientate herself, she took off briskly towards Ossemsley, her heart full of hope but desperately afraid that she would be caught out after hours, an unforgivable sin on the farm.

It took her just over an hour in the end, the old manor house looming out of the darkness as she approached.

She saw immediately that the driveway was guarded and swore under her breath. Silently, she stole to the left of the house, along the perimeter of the stone wall surrounding it, until she spotted a tree that looked easy enough to climb. Within a few moments, she was sitting with her back to the trunk and her feet braced upon a thick branch while she stared over the wall.

Her heart sank.

She could see a line of wire fencing inside the wall, and beyond that, a series of huts, presumably housing the PoWs. While she might be able to drop from the tree over the wall, the fence was high, and it did not take good night vision to spot the barbed wire coiled viciously along the top.

There was no way in, and sick at heart, Elsie began the long trudge home, her steps weighed down with the dashed hopes of the night.

***

The next day, Elsie was at pains to cover her fatigue, and did her best to work diligently. Her efforts did not go unnoticed, and at eleven o'clock she was called over by Mrs Pidgley.

'We've been told to take apples down to the PoWs.' She sniffed. 'Apparently, they need the vitamins to work, but why we should waste our food on them beggars belief. Can you take the cart once you've loaded it up? You're good with the horses?'

Elsie smiled outwardly at the praise, and inwardly at the opportunity.

She accepted with alacrity and hitched up the horses as soon as she had swung the crates of apples up into the back of the cart.

Driving them slowly down the lane, she was stunned by the level of activity which was going on around her. Men everywhere, and a long runway with interconnecting pathways stretched across the heathland, on a far bigger scale than she had imagined.

She drove on towards the line of Nissan huts where she had been told to deliver the apples, conscious of the men's eyes on her as she approached.

There was a silence as she jumped down from the cart, but as she went to the back to unload the crates, a voice spoke softly behind her.

'Let me help you with that.'

Without turning, she knew it was Josef.

'Are you all right?' she asked and was relieved to hear him chuckle.

'As all right as can be expected for a prisoner.'

'I want to see you properly. I need to talk to you and find out how you really are,' she muttered, near tears at the familiarity of his voice. 'I know where you're staying, but I can't get in.' Her voice cracked.

'No, you can't,' he replied, and Elsie was surprised to hear laughter in his voice, 'but I, I can get out.'

'Can we meet somewhere?' she asked incredulously but jumped as another man walked round the back of the cart and chastised Josef for 'monopolising the lady'. Suddenly there was a little crowd around them and their moment seemed to be over.

Over, but not lost. As strong hands reached out to help her back onto the cart, a soft whisper in her ear,

'Be south of the wall tonight. I'll be there.'

Chapter 20

Love and Loss

And oh God, he was there. There, moments after she arrived, his shape appearing stealthily out of the shadows and astonishing her despite the fact that every sense of her being was straining to watch for him.

They might never had foreseen what they were to become, years before, but walking into his arms now seemed as natural as if they had always been together, as if four years had not passed since sleeping under the tarp on the boat on the long haul back from Dunkirk. They clung to one another for a long moment, and then she pulled away to look up at him.

'How…?'

But he was already silencing her with a kiss, his lips hungry against hers and his arms holding her tight.

'I have many ways out,' he whispered. 'I have made myself useful around here. And they know I have no desire to escape.'

It was his turn to pull away now, looking hard into her eyes. 'You know the invasion is going to happen soon?'

She nodded, not trusting herself to speak. Seeing Josef, feeling his lips for the first time, speaking of the forbidden all made her shiver, both with excitement and fear.

'What will happen to you?' she asked.

'I don't know,' he answered honestly. If the Allies win, maybe I'll be deported back to Germany. If they lose...' He stopped.

It was Elsie's turn to reach up to him now, stopping his lips with her own.

'Then we don't want to waste any time.'

***

Monique watched Elsie surreptitiously over the next few weeks, spotting the lines of fatigue around her eyes and her drawn complexion.

'We're due some leave,' she announced one morning after they had finished breakfast and were heading out to the horses. 'Mrs Pidgley told me earlier.'

'How long?' asked Elsie, surprised, and when Monique answered 'three days,' she smiled, but Monique could see it seemed to cost her an effort.

'Shall we go to see Mum and Daisy?' she said, and Monique smiled. 'Where else would we go?'

The little cottage in Mudeford seemed unchanged apart from the black out which was now permanently taped to the windows at the front of the house. Slipping round the back, Elsie smiled to see that the kitchen door was open, and her baby sister crouched in the back yard with a bucket full of crabs. The little girl was staring intently into her bucket, and with her wild curly hair blowing in her eyes, she did not see Elsie watching her. She winked at Monique, who was profoundly pleased to see the mischievous glow that had been missing from her face of late.

'Let's sneak up and surprise her.'

Daisy was pleased to see them both squealing as Elsie scooped her up in her arms.

'You must be eating too many crabs. You're so big now.'

Daisy laughed. 'We can't eat these crabs. They're too little,' she protested. 'But I've been fishing with Daniel and I've catched some big fish.'

'Caught,' Elsie corrected automatically as her heart lurched.

She hadn't seen Daniel for over a year. Last time she and Monique had left, he was out fishing for the whole weekend, ostensibly to make the best of the spring tides, but probably, she guessed to avoid her.

Her heart ached at that thought. That she and Daniel could have lost their easy friendship was so hard to bear, yet she had no real idea how to breach the rift between them.

She knew that would be even harder now. She had been seeing Josef almost every other night for the past three months, meeting in a little clearing they had found halfway between Ossemsley and the farm, a clearing marked by a tall silver birch trunk long since blasted by lightning, its scarred silver an easy landmark against the moon. She was utterly exhausted but couldn't bear to stop their nightly trysts in the dark of the moon, as hungry to see him as he was for her.

They knew there was little time left. The runway extensions were complete and the whole area a hive of activity. More and more planes seemed to be there every day, and the atmosphere of urgency was palpable.

How could she face Daniel and not let him know about Josef? How could she face her once dearest friend and not explain that she was in love?

***

But, in the end, Daniel came to her.

Daisy had, in fact, been fishing with Daniel that very day, and he was already invited around to share their booty, albeit not knowing that Monique and Elsie would be home.

He stopped short when he came in the kitchen door, then held out his arms and said simply, 'All right?'

The sight of his shock of dirty blond hair was so achingly familiar, although the crutch still jarred on Elsie's nerves. She went straight to him, and for the first time in a long time, they hugged each other, hard. The warmth of their friendship reignited through this heartfelt touch.

'I'm all right.'

The next day, Elsie woke in her old bedroom and smiled at the sunlight dancing from the reflection off the waves outside.

She rolled over and saw that Monique had risen early, and when she glanced at the clock, she was shocked to see that it read almost half past ten. She had slept for twelve straight hours, and she grinned when she admitted to herself, she probably needed to catch up on the lack of sleep from the past weeks.

Padding downstairs in her bare feet, she entered the kitchen to find Monique nursing a cup of acorn coffee. The smell of it tuned Elsie's stomach, so she ran herself some cold water from the tap instead and joined her at the table.

'Your mum has taken Daisy out to run off some steam.'

Elsie smiled. She loved it when Monique used such quintessentially English expressions with her fading, but still noticeable French accent.

'It was good to see Daniel last night,' she said. 'I'm so glad we were able to come home for a while.'

Monique's face darkened a little, and Elsie felt guilty. 'I'm so sorry,' she said, 'that was really thoughtless…'

Monique cut her off. 'Elsie. My home is gone now, the farm will have been run into the ground by those bloody Bosch. I'm just glad I have you, and all this…' She faltered as she waved her arm out at the view of the harbour, and her eyes filled with tears.

Elsie got up and went round the table to hug her. 'Let's go for a walk,' she said briskly. 'We could both do with a chance of scene and some sea air.'

She scooped up the cups and went to scrape the crumbs from the remains of Monique's breakfast into the dustbin, but as she lifted the lid, the smell of fish assailed her nostrils from last night's dinner. For a moment, her head swam, then gagging, she dashed to the door with her hand clapped over her mouth, just making it in time to be violently sick in the yard.

***

Monique walked next to her without saying a word.

There was nothing to be said, the enormity of the situation hitting them both and rendering them speechless.

After she had stopped vomiting, Monique took her up to their bedroom and sat her down. Together, they counted backwards and only then did Elsie finally accept that her period was at least three weeks late. She had been so caught up in Josef, so exhausted by meeting him so frequently, that all else had slipped her mind.

All rhyme and reason.

Eventually, Monique took her out for some air. Glancing sideways at her ashen face, she asked gently,

'May I ask whose it is?'

Elsie shook her head furiously. 'I just can't tell you,' she said. 'I'm sorry, but I just can't.'

'Elsie, you saved my life once. You can tell me anything.'

But Elsie simply shook her head and walked faster, so that Monique had to trot to catch her up.

'What do you think you should do?' she ventured, but Elsie shook her head again.

'I can't talk about this now,' she muttered. 'I have to deal with this in my own time.'

'Elsie, you don't have time. You're going to need help! We work on the land!' Monique burst out, but Elsie stopped dead and turned on her, her face full of rage.

'This is my problem, not yours. Just leave me alone and let me think!'

Turning on her heel, she stalked back to the house and by the time Monique had caught up with her, she was in bed again with the blanket firmly pulled up over her head to shut out the world.

***

She lay in the dark, her hand resting on her stomach. Unknown, unthought of, but a life, nonetheless, resting under her fingertips.

Josef's child.

Her hands holding her heart, listening for an answering beat. Life, life beneath her hands, life created from the very force of love.

Her lips curved in a sudden smile. This was her secret for now, but she knew what his reaction would be. Josef craved a normal life. He craved family. He would be so happy.

She rolled over, more carefully than usual, and found Monique's eyes fixed upon her from the twin bed they had long since installed across the little room.

She felt so close to Monique in so many ways, and desperately wanted to tell her what she had asked. But she was unable to banish Monique's rejection of Josef after he had given himself away with his tortured sleep talking during that long and fateful night. It had been plain to both Daniel and Elsie how close Monique and Josef had become before they had plucked them from the sea, which made her utter repulsion and rejection of her companion all the more shocking.

'Are you all right?' whispered Monique, and Elsie's eyes filled with ready tears.

'I'm all right. Just taking stock, really.' she paused. 'I will tell you, Monique, but I just need to get used to the idea myself. And…' She hesitated again. 'I need to tell him first.'

Monique nodded, satisfied for the time being. 'What about the farm? And Mrs Pidgley?'

Elsie sucked her breath in and let it out in a long slow hiss, doing her utmost to quell the rising nausea that seemed to mirror every anxious thought.

'Can you try to cover me with some of the heavier stuff?' she ventured, and the tears fell finally when Monique swung her legs out of bed and enveloped her in a long hug. 'Of course I will. For as long as it is possible, I will do everything I can.'

***

She was as good as her word.

Each morning, she would sneak extra breakfast into the pockets of her overalls, knowing that Elsie would need it later but couldn't stomach it at sunrise.

Each day, she let Elsie drive the horses while she loaded and unloaded the cart. While Elsie was happy on her knees weeding around the vegetables, Monique would scoop up whatever she dug up and swing it away even before Elsie protested that she could have lifted it.

One afternoon, they took a short break and sat, side by side, on the back of the cart, their legs swinging, and their faces turned towards the sun.

She glanced surreptitiously at Elsie, then asked curiously, 'Can I ask you something? Have you told him yet?'

Elsie stiffened, a cloud crossing her sunny features. 'Not yet,' she answered, eventually, and Monique bit her lip, guilty at spoiling the calm.

'But you're starting to show a bit,' she muttered, and Elsie turned on her, her eyes flashing.

'I am well aware of that,' she hissed. 'But I haven't been able to see him since we came back from leave! I don't know where he's gone!'

Monique stared at her, puzzled. 'But why…' She drew to a halt at the sight of the conflict in her friend's face. 'Does he live near here?' she tried again.

'He was staying nearby. I went to see him, but' – Elsie paused and took a shaky breath – 'but he wasn't there.'

Elsie had been sixteen times.

Sixteen times, she had crept out in the dark of night, sixteen times she had hiked in silence to the clearing she knew so well, guided by the sentinel of the silver birch in the moonlight.

Once, in desperation, she had walked all the way to Ossemsley, climbed the tree with difficulty compared to the way she had swung herself up easily so many months ago.

He was not there, and she couldn't make him out among the truckloads of men that continued to trundle in and out of what was now, clearly, an enormous airfield behind the farm.

Monique reached out and squeezed her hand tightly. 'Maybe you could write to him?' She suggested. 'But in the meantime, I'll help you let out your overalls a bit, so it's not so obvious they're getting tight.'

***

In the end, it was Mrs Pidgley, not Monique, who helped Elsie sort her overalls out.

She stood outside their bedroom the next morning and waited. When Monique came out first, she went to say 'good morning' but Mrs Pidgley stopped her with fingers to her lips.

'I need to have a quiet word,' she mouthed, and knocked gently on the wooden door, lifting the latch when Elsie called, 'Come in.'

Elsie went to scramble up when she saw who her visitor was, but Mrs Pidgley shook her head firmly. 'Rest a bit longer, Elsie. You need all the rest you can get.'

'I'm fine,' she protested, but again Mrs Pidgley shook her head.

'You're not "fine",' she answered. 'You're pregnant.'

Elsie stared at her, aghast, then her eyes filled with tears at the warm smile from the farmer's wife.

'Love, I'm not deaf and blind,' she said, simply. 'I've heard you being sick, and I know you can't face your breakfast. Now, tell me whose it is, and we can see about getting you sorted out.'

Elsie couldn't help herself and burst out crying. Somehow, the relief of a mother figure loosened her tongue, and in broken sobs, the story came out as the sun rose, picking out the dust motes swirling through the attic bedroom as if everything was normal and the world hadn't gone mad.

Eventually, she laid back down on the bed, too exhausted by telling her own story and weeping to carry on.

Mrs Pidgley took a long breath. 'So, you've got yourself in a bit of a fix, then?' she murmured. 'But Elsie, I won't let you go through this on your own. You can have the baby here. What you do afterwards is up to you. But if I were you, I wouldn't say a word about the father. I don't think many people would understand.'

Elsie nodded, overwhelmed by her generosity. 'I won't tell a soul.'

But unbeknownst to them both, someone else did know. Standing silently on the landing outside the door, Monique had heard every word, and with her face set like stone, she turned and tiptoed silently down the stairs and out into the fresh air.

***

Two weeks later, they were due more leave, and reluctantly this time, they left together for the cottage in Mudeford.

Monique could hardly bring herself to meet Elsie's eye, and Elsie, aware of the new strain between them but not being sure of the reason, did not know how to reach her.

She was also bracing herself for the conversations to be had, one which she was dreading more than the other. Telling her mother would be no great barrier, as she had long ago ceased to be a mother figure for her, she did not feel constrained by normal social etiquette and niceties. But telling Daniel – her heart constricted – ah, telling Daniel, was enough to break her courage before she even arrived.

As they opened the kitchen door and walked in, Betsy jumped up to give them both a hug, then stopped dead when she saw Elsie's waistline.

'I'll take Daisy for a walk,' announced Monique, and scooped the squealing girl up into her arms, diplomatically exiting as soon as she could.

Betsy looked at her daughter, then said, carefully, 'well I can hardly throw stones, can I?'

And all of a sudden, they were both in tears, mother and daughter, estranged and brought together by the events of two world wars, flotsam and jetsam on an unfeeling ocean. Two women who had faced hardship and made their own individual decisions to survive.

Come what may.

Some time later, Betsy sat stroking the damp hair from Elsie's brow as they sat, like survivors of a storm, motionless in front of the hot stove.

'Do you want me to tell Daniel?' Betsy asked and was rewarded by a long groan.

'Should I tell him the truth, Mum?'

Betsy paused for a long moment.

'I think not. If he thinks it's a farm boy working the land, I think he'll forgive you. But if he knows it's Josef's child…?'

She petered out, uncertainly.

Elsie nodded. 'That's what I think, too. I'll tell him later, Mum. Will you wait up for me?'

Betsy smiled, her heart lurching that her daughter needed her, needed her in a way that she could understand and help.

In the end, as always, Daniel made it easy for her.

Despite his first, clearly visible shock, he swiftly drew breath and asked, as ever, 'All right?'

The familiarity made them both laugh, then Elsie cried. Daniel's arms going around her instinctively, just like in those first days when she cut school to sail out with him to fish in open water.

Before, when they had been each other's everything.

Hours later, he asked, 'Come out with me?'

And, like some kind of breath from the halcyon days of their first friendship, the wind caught their sails, and they ghosted out on the evening tide, a world to catch up on and a friendship to carry them through.

***

Betsy got up early and stoked up the stove, Daisy dancing around 'helping'. Seeing her daughter's irrepressible high spirits, Betsy sighed, then asked her to go out and 'catch crabs for tea.'

Child duly dispatched, she readied herself to take breakfast up to Elsie, her maternal instinct yearning to look after her now. Whether it was because of the guilt for leaving her as a child, or simply empathy, woman to woman, she needed to perform this simple act of kindness for her daughter.

She jumped as Monique entered the kitchen. Somehow, she hadn't even given a thought to the quiet French girl who had become so much part of her wartime, war-torn family.

She took a deep breath, asked, 'Do you know who the father is?'

Monique shook her head firmly. Lied. 'She won't tell anyone. I think it must be a local boy.'

Betsy nodded, relieved. She had grown to love Monique these past long years, but she knew she had a dark side, an unforgiving streak that wouldn't stand reason or explanation.

Better that she did not know.

Not knowing that, as Monique turned her face away to pour the tea, she was thinking precisely the same thoughts.

Better that no one knew what she knew.

***

Daniel sat in the stern of his boat, splicing a line which had begun to fray with age. Checking that it still ran easily through the fairlead, he sat back and squinted across the narrow stretch of water between his mooring and Elsie's home.

That she was pregnant, he could understand. That she wouldn't name the father hurt him more than he could say. Why could she not tell him? Who was she trying to protect? And from what he could gather from her tears, the man was now gone and no longer part of her life, a fact which he found impossible to forgive. He had learnt from a young age to live up to your own responsibilities, taking over his father's boat when he got too ill to fish, keeping the money coming into their home in the months before he died.

To just up and leave, leave a girl whom he must have professed to have loved… He shuddered with suppressed rage and vowed that he would do everything in his power to look after Elsie and the baby when it came.

***

The night the baby came, the Allies invaded France. Elsie lay in her bed that morning, her hands resting on her swollen belly, tracking every movement, every shift of position, every kick. On rising, she moved off slowly in the direction of the stables, and as she went to throw the halter over the big cart horse, she felt a sharp twinge of pain.

She paused for a moment and straightened up carefully. 'Not yet, baby,' she murmured, I have to get these boys hitched up.' She had begun talking to her bump from the first moment that she had felt the first flicker of movement under her probing fingertips, the swelling suddenly becoming a real little being in her mind's eye.

The second twinge made her gasp, and Monique, who had just come to take the lead reins from her, whirled around to look at her. This time, Elsie did not straighten up. She was too intent on focusing on the pain and keeping from crying out.

'Is it coming?' Monique asked, and Elsie met her eye and nodded, too overwhelmed with fear and excitement to speak.

Monique took her by the hand and led her gently back to the farmhouse, where Mrs Pidgley took over. Casting an experienced eye over the frightened young woman before her, she counselled her to keep moving, to stay on her feet as long as she could. She kept Elsie going around the farmhouse with as many light chores as she could think of, and when she judged the time was right, she began to fill the tin bath by the stove in the kitchen and helped her bathe.

The pains took over after that.

Elsie did not know it, but Mrs Pidgley took her into her own bedroom, where she and Monique had prepared the bed for this moment. As Monique boiled the kettle and handed Mrs Pidgley the first of the hot towels, the next stage of labour hit Elsie as the aeroplanes began to take off from the airfield behind them, the waves of sound rolling over her as a fitting backdrop to the pain.

And as the last plane lifted its nose into the sky and headed for Normandy and liberation, the baby slipped out in a hot rush of fresh agony, to be caught by the expert hands of Mrs Pidgley and rested upon Elsie's breast for the very first time.

**

The next few days passed in a milky blur for Elsie, days while, on the world stage, the Allies swept through Normandy to take back France from the Third Reich.

The baby was a girl, with the softest skin Elsie had ever felt, and the clearest, grey eyes. Her hair, what she had of it, was light brown and downy to the touch, and Elsie spent hours inhaling the top of her head and feeling it flutter against her face.

She was utterly beautiful, and in Elsie's eyes, the spitting image of Josef, except that her hair began to curl from the moment Mrs Pidgley bathed her for the first time.

'She's beautiful,' she murmured, as she handed her back to the exhausted girl lying spent on the bed. 'But don't let her feed all night. She'll sap you of your strength.'

Elsie smiled wanly. She had, indeed, been feeding her for hours most nights. Her little insistent mouth was hard to ignore, tugging away at her breast as she would settle slowly, finally satiated with her mother's milk. She was a peaceful baby, but slow to feed, each time taking an hour or more, during which time often both mother and child would fall asleep, then jolt awake, back to the job in hand.

'What will you call her?' ventured Mrs Pidgley, curiously.

Elsie paused, looking down at the little head asleep against her chest.

'Ursula,' she said, finally, and firmly. 'She needs a strong name for these times.'

And Mrs Pidgley nodded, understanding that this child might also need a name that was equally English and German in these shifting sands of wartime.

Chapter 21

Betrayal

Monique took the letter that Elsie wrote and delivered it personally to Betsy.

Betsy jumped up as she entered the door, her face paling at the sight of Monique, then flushing at her nod and reassuring smile. Betsy was overjoyed at the news that her daughter had pulled through, that the baby was well, and that little Daisy would now have a niece to meet and help care for.

'What does she look like?' she asked excitedly and was rewarded by a dark look from Monique.

'Like Elsie, but her eyes are grey,' she answered shortly, doing her best to banish the memory of that night at the farm.

But later, tucked up in the bedroom overlooking the harbour that she used to share with her friend, she dreamt again of the men coming for her, those hard, grey eyes, soldier after soldier forcing her down until her back bled on the barn floor. She awoke shaking and panting with fright, her stomach twisting with revulsion.

Aware that Elsie had noticed her inability to hold little Ursula, couldn't bear to look her in the eye.

Could not believe nor forgive that her friend had lain, voluntarily, with the bloody Bosch.

A knock at her door made her jump violently, a sudden intrusion into her own personal world of the past. Wrenched back to tonight, Monique sat up and answered.

'Are you all right?' asked Betsy tactfully. 'I thought I heard you tossing and turning a bit.'

'I couldn't sleep.'

'I have a lot of trouble sleeping, too. I have a sleeping draft my doctor gave me. Would you like some?'

'To be honest,' Monique said slowly. 'I haven't been sleeping for ages. I suppose I couldn't have a little now, and take some with me?' A thread of an idea began to connect in her mind.

'Of course, love,' answered Betsy. 'I've got two bottles, anyway. I'll go and get you something now.'

And in a few moments, she reappeared with a little bottle, a teaspoon and a glass of water.

'There you go. One spoonful now, and a little bottle to get you through the next few weeks, get your bounce back.'

Monique smiled gratefully. 'This will help me more than you know.'

***

The next morning, Monique rose early, full of conviction that the idea, which had come to her in those early hours of the morning, was going to make things right.

She watched from the kitchen window, and the moment that she saw Daniel preparing to go out to the boat, she ran out to greet him.

He whirled at the sound of her voice.

'Is Elsie all right? Has the baby come?'

She nodded. 'It came. It's a girl, they're both all right. But, Daniel…' Her voice faltered, then went on, stronger than before. 'She's decided she is going to give it up.'

Daniel stared. 'For adoption? Is she sure?'

'She's sure.'

'But we can all help her. I'm willing to do anything, and so is Betsy. They can move back here. She can't be expected to do war work with a newborn,' he said. The protest clear in his voice.

Monique looked down at her hands. 'She thinks it's for the best.' she lied. 'And she doesn't want anyone to try to stop her.'

When Monique left the next day, she took two letters with her, one from Betsy, with Daisy's name laboriously added in pencil with hundreds of 'kisses for baby', and another one, tightly sealed, from Daniel.

As she left Mudeford, she gazed at the sea view which she had come to love so much, and with a last look at the sunlight glowing on the ancient Priory, she shredded them both and dropped the pieces into the ebbing tide.

***

Six long weeks later, Monique took delivery of the telegram from the boy on the bicycle and slipped off to the barn to read it.

We confirm that we will take the baby in. Stop. Once you have signed the papers, please understand you cannot change your mind. Stop. You will not be able to see the baby again. Stop. If this is acceptable to you, we can arrange to collect her. Stop. Rest assured we will look after her. Stop.

***

That night, Ursula was unsettled, and Elsie paced back and forth, back and forth, jiggling her on her shoulder and trying to settle her. The fretful child seemed to be calmed by feeding, but as soon as Elsie burped her and went to lay her down, the crying would start again, insistent and setting both Monique and Elsie on edge.

'I'm sorry.' Elsie burst out eventually. 'I'm doing my best.'

Monique smiled. 'That's the only thing any of us can do.'

She padded quietly downstairs and a few minutes later, reappeared with a mug of hot milk.

'This is for you. It might make you feel a bit calmer.'

Elsie smiled her gratitude, then grimaced. 'The milk is a bit on the turn. But it smells good, and the warmth is lovely, thank you.'

Monique watched out of the corner of her eye.

Elsie drank every drop.

'You know, she might need weaning,' remarked Monique casually. 'I picked up the infant rationing card last week when I went to the Post Office. It just crossed my mind that she might be needing more soon.'

Elsie smiled, gratefully. 'I was starting to wonder the same thing. What do I have to do to get the extra ration?'

Monique slipped the papers over to her friend, noticing how heavy her lids seemed now. 'You just need to sign here.'

***

In the years to come, she would remember it in the passage of heartbeats.

Beat.

Waking to see the sunlight filtering through the little window, the dust motes dancing to their own tune.

Beat.

Realising that she had slept deeply, and slept in.

Beat.

Feeling the wet soaking through the front of her flannel nightshirt, realising she was leaking milk from aching breasts.

Beat.

Seeing that the crib was empty.

Beat.

Understanding, as the last beat echoed like a death knell in her chest, that her baby was gone.

***

Mrs Pidgley straightened her shoulders and pushed her hair tiredly back out of her eyes. The doctor had just left, leaving Elsie heavily sedated. She had screamed all day, utterly hysterical, utterly distraught.

She went quietly down the stairs and met Monique in the kitchen.

'What ever made her decide to go for adoption?' she asked. 'I wished she had talked it through with me. And what made her change her mind again?'

Monique paused, knowing that what she said now needed to ring absolutely true.

'Her mother wrote and told her not to darken her door by bringing a baby home. So, we talked and talked, and Elsie agreed that she needed to give' – she paused, not able to say Ursula's name – 'needed to give her up. But now it's happened, she can't accept it.'

'Is it too late?' pressed Mrs Pidgley, and Monique nodded.

'The sisters told me that once she had signed the papers, the decision couldn't be changed.'

Monique crossed her fingers behind her back and waited.

Mrs Pidgley sighed. 'It's probably for the best in the long run,' she agreed. 'I just didn't see it coming, that's all.'

Monique breathed out silently. 'She didn't want to talk about it. She told me the subject is closed.'

Later on that night, Elsie lay sleepless and staring at Monique's back.

'Monique?' She breathed. 'I don't remember anything. I don't remember signing anything. I don't remember asking you to take her away.'

Monique rolled over and met her eye. 'You've been so tired,' she murmured. 'But you will remember soon. You told me you couldn't cope, and that you couldn't keep her.'

Elsie's eyes were cold.

'I don't remember.'

Chapter 22

VE Day: Farewells and a Return to Dunkirk

'Listen.'

The girls stood stock still, resting on their tool handles as they tried to make sense of what they were hearing.

For the first time in six long years, the sound of bells was brought to them on the breeze, at the same time as Daniel, Betsy and Daisy went to stand out by the harbourside to listen to the bells of the ancient Priory beginning to sound.

'Is it over?'

Elsie and Monique looked at one another, and suddenly both were crying, arms around each other as the import of what they were hearing began to sink in.

The contact between them was the first in a very long time. Elsie had withdrawn her open and easy friendship, never outwardly accusing Monique, but her new-found mistrust clear on her face.

Monique explained to her, again and again, that she had been struggling from Baby Blues, that she had begged Monique to take Ursula away. That she had implored her to do it before she did something she would regret.

All Elsie could do was remember a mind-numbing tiredness, a blur over those early days almost blocking out her vision of those beautiful grey eyes and wispy curls.

But now, for one moment in time, they hugged and wept, not realising yet that the war that had brought them together was about to blow them apart.

***

Life in Mudeford was never going to be the same.

Betsy died.

When Elsie returned, she found her mother tired and withdrawn, and unwilling to discuss the grandchild that she had never seen. Elsie tried to talk to her, needing to explain that, somehow, Baby Blues had led her to do a terrible thing, making an irrevocable mistake, but each time, Betsy looked away with unforgiving eyes.

'I've brought Daisy up on my own. Why couldn't you even try?'

And each time, the nail was driven a little further in, Elsie wincing with pain and striving to remember what had happened, what had made her lose her mind.

Then, slowly, Elsie saw that her mother was ill, growing thinner each day as her bitterness and disappointment in her own daughter grew. One day, she walked in on her mother accidentally as she was dressing and stopped dead at the sight of her scraggy body, ribs poking through skin as thin as paper.

'Mum,' she cried. 'You must go to the doctor.'

'I've been, Elsie. There's nothing they can do.'

Elsie gazed at her, uncomprehendingly.

'Nothing? But what is it?'

Betsy drew a breath and looked directly at her. 'It's cancer. In my womb. There's nothing they can do.'

And over the coming weeks while her daughter nursed her and attended to her every need until the day she slipped away from this life, there was no rapprochement, no forgiveness by the mother who would never forgive nor forget the terrible decision that had torn their family apart.

***

In the end, Daniel took Monique home.

Elsie threw herself into looking after Daisy, trying to become the big sister she had never really been there to be, as well as stepping into her mother's shoes. Each day, they looked for news of Jack, expecting word at any time.

Monique knew that she was not wanted, nor needed. Something had broken between her and Elsie that a few hugs on VE Day could not repair, and she found herself longing for home, trying to cope with the waves of homesickness by taking long walks along the harbour every day. Murmuring 'ducks… *canards*. Moorhens… *poules d'eau*,' then realising she needed to think hard to find the French words after so many years being utterly immersed in English.

Daniel knew that the rift between them was deep, but believed it was the guilt about giving Ursula up for adoption that stopped Elsie from talking to Monique. He had begun to feel sorry for the tall French girl, her loneliness clear to see. One evening, he saw her on the edge of the water as he was mooring up, and when he waved, she hopped down off the wall and began to wade out to him, scooping her skirt up off her brown legs out of the water.

'Permission to come aboard?'

He smiled and reached down to give her a hand over the gunwale.

She sat down on the warm boards, and for a moment, Daniel remembered Elsie doing just the same when they had first met.

'Will you take me back?' she asked suddenly, and he stared at her.

'I have no idea how to get home, and I have no money. But if you took me…' Her voice faded as the tears came.

Daniel sat down opposite her, sighed, and took her hand. 'Can you give me some time to prepare? It's cold at this time of year and Dunkirk was so hard, we hadn't prepared at all, and we need to be properly provisioned this time, especially…' His voice cracked. 'Especially as I'll be sailing home alone.'

Monique looked at him and realised then how dear to her he had become over the war years, the boy who had saved her had become her friend, there for her in every leave she had taken, here for her now when she needed to leave. That there was nothing she could want more than sailing away from it all with him, now her closest friend, days alone at sea and then walking home to Solange and the remains of her family farm.

'Let's make a list.'

***

Elsie watched her with cold eyes, and Monique turned away.

She had slept badly that night, waking again and again to a half-dreamt, half-remembered baby's cry, her breasts, even now, leaking milk as her eyes leaked hot tears.

A hard little head, resting against her breast, first insistently and tugging at her for more, then heavy and damp against her as Ursula would slip into sleep.

Gazing down at her head, seeing the curve of her eyelashes, and shifting slightly to allow the film of milk between her soft little cheek and her breast to dry.

Seeing Josef in one instant, herself in the next, her breath catching at the momentous love that was growing within her.

And then, then a heaviness, a terrible lassitude, a few days she seemed to have lost somewhere, a few days when she couldn't seem to cope. A few nights when Monique had comforted her, fed her hot milk, and helped her to bed when the tiredness took hold.

A bone tiredness, swamping her and confusing her, memories and thoughts flitting in and out of her mind to be lost on the night breeze. Monique talking her through, cajoling her, supporting her. Talking to her about weaning, getting her to sign papers for Ursula's infant ration. Telling her that she probably didn't have enough milk to satiate her own baby.

Knowing that something was terribly wrong, but not being able to sweep aside the cobwebs from her memories of those few days to see the truth, although, somewhere in her heart, she knew that she had not willingly, knowingly given up her up her own flesh and blood, borne of the man whom she loved, body and soul. The man she wept for at nights, along with the loss of her first-born daughter.

***

Daniel and Monique left three days later, when the weather was fair and the wind favourable for sailing east.

Neither of them having a clear idea of the exact destination but intending to recreate what Elsie and Daniel had managed those long years before, sailing east until the Channel narrowed, then turning south when the wind allowed.

Daniel sat quietly, watching Monique sleep under the tarp in the bow as he steered gently downwind, the sails goose-winged in the light of the dawn. At this point of sail, they went with the wind, so the air seemed still, and he rolled his shoulders and relaxed into the early warmth of the rising sun. He was relishing the long passage; since Elsie and Monique had returned, he had felt duty-bound to stay close, especially in those terrible days when it was suddenly clear to all that Betsy was dying. He shut his eyes for a moment, letting his hand relax on the tiller.

He was truly proud of Elsie, of the way that she had nursed her mother into and through her final days yet finding time to comfort and also entertain little Daisy.

He shook his head again against the thought that kept popping up, unbidden, into his mind.

Elsie was a natural carer.

She had love, support, and friends, as well as a mother who would never have judged, as she too had once been judged.

So why, why on Earth would she have given up her daughter?

***

Leaving Ramsgate brought back a flood of memories. This time, the little harbour was quiet, but in Daniel's mind's eye, he could see the boats moored like sardines all those years ago, fishermen and old men preparing to set sail, daring and determined to rescue sons and brothers. The light in Elsie's eyes as she had turned to him and told him her plan. The fear and the desperation of that long day and night, following and losing the trail of little ships as their little boat fell behind, then hearing the cries of the wounded as the first boats began to return.

And then, finding Monique and Josef, rescuing the least expected but equally desperate.

Daniel sighed, remembering Josef's quiet dignity on the day he had taken him to the police station, the tall German walking steadily but slowly to match Daniel's stiff gait. Handing himself in to the bemused local bobby, who had never seen a German, let alone had to take charge of a prisoner of war. Turning and offering his hand, meeting his eye, and asking him to please, please look after the girls. Both girls. He had taken his hand and promised.

After Monique had prepared their frugal evening meal, land came into sight.

She couldn't take her eyes off it, looming closer and closer but agonisingly slowly, her beloved France.

Her eyes filled with tears, and, seeing her emotion, Daniel hove to, letting the sails hold the boat still and steady as he took her hand.

'Talk to me,' he said.

'It's been so long. I have no idea what I'm going back to, if there is anything to go back to at all. My farm…'

Her voice trailed off and Daniel hugged her hard, feeling her body shaking against his.

'What happened, Monique?' he asked eventually. 'What happened that made you leave?'

She pulled away. 'The Germans came. Isn't that enough?'

The way her face closed told him that there was more to it than that, as he had always suspected, just as he knew now that she wouldn't tell him or anyone else the reason for her flight.

'How do you want to do this?' he asked gently and was rewarded by a smile and a truly Gallic shrug.

'I think I just want to make it simple. Just run the boat up into the shallows and I'll walk ashore. I only have my backpack, so I can just jump. I don't think I could cope with a long goodbye.'

Her eyes filled with tears again, remembering how Josef had taken her hand and run into the sea on that terrible night that had saved their lives. And Daniel caught his breath, looking at her, remembering how he and Elsie had reached over and pulled two people aboard, two people who had changed their lives.

And suddenly, they were crying and kissing, and as they made love in the bottom of the boat, the one was remembering a tall, blond German who had fed her, looked after her and spurred her ever onwards, while the other was thinking of a girl with curly chestnut hair who had saved him when he was injured and helped him find his way through the dark days to acceptance of his lot.

It was as natural a way as any, for two friends thrown together by war and separated by peace, to say goodbye.

Much later, Daniel pushed his boat back out of the shallows and turned to look, one last time, at the tall French girl, who had jumped lightly onto the sandbank and had started walking away as soon as she found her feet.

Monique paused when she reached the beach and turned for the last time.

One wave, and she was gone.

Chapter 23

Hot Milk and Memories

Elsie sat on the window seat on the tiny landing outside Daisy's room, watching the light dying over the harbour. Daisy's sobs had finally calmed to exhausted snuffles while she had lain holding her, and eventually she had extricated herself, aching and stiff, from cuddling the bereft little girl.

She missed Daniel, and if she was honest, she missed Monique too, more than she could say. It had been a lifetime, six long war years that had brought them together, spending every hour of the day and night in each other's company since that fateful meeting in the seas of Dunkirk.

Tears prickled, and she walked quietly downstairs and splashed her face in the kitchen sink, not wanting to awaken tomorrow with dry, raw eyes again. She stoked up the stove and sat reading for a little while, hoping to feel sleepy enough to get a better night tonight. After an hour, she yawned and decided to turn in.

The night was cool and fresh, and she lay for a while watching the pattern of the waves dancing in the moonlight, reflecting on her bedroom ceiling, just as she used to with Jack when they were children.

Jack. She rolled over, her shoulder uncomfortable against the hard mattress, and began to worry.

Why had they not had word?

Nearly eight months had passed since VE Day, most of the troops were back already, yet not a single letter, no telegram. Nothing.

She shifted again, realising that all chance of sleep were now gone.

Suddenly, she heard a little cry, and was instantly on her feet, listening outside the room that Daisy had always shared with their mother. Daisy was tossing and turning, and little sobs were slipping from her lips even in her sleep. Elsie's heart broke as she looked down at her. Yet another little girl who had lost both her parents, a father unknown and a mother gone. Another spoil of war.

She crouched for a while, stroking Daisy's hot little forehead until she seemed to settle.

As she turned to leave the room, her foot caught against a box jutting out from under her mother's bed, and as she tripped, the lid slipped off. Immediately, her eyes lit on a stash of medicines, mostly pain killers from those terrible last weeks, and she stooped to pick them up, knowing that she should have removed them from harm's way long ago.

In the light of the kitchen, she began to sort through the boxes, stashing those she thought might be useful for fever relief in case she or Daisy became ill, putting others she did not recognise aside to return to her doctor in good time.

It was then that she saw the sleeping draft.

She held it up and shook it. There was at least half a bottle left. She paused for a moment, then the need for sleep decided her. She took a bottle of milk out of the cold pantry and poured it into the smallest saucepan, popping it onto the stove to heat up while she put the other medicines out of reach.

Soon, she padded back upstairs with the bottle in one hand and her hot milk in the other, pausing for a while outside Daisy's bedroom until she was satisfied with the calm breathing coming from within.

Scrambling into bed, Elsie twitched the curtains shut, determined to have a good rest. Opening the bottle, she sniffed its contents and wrinkled her nose. She poured the dose into the spoon, and as she swallowed it back, the sharp taste pervaded her senses, and quickly took a big gulp of milk to wash it down.

Then sat bolt upright, her head reeling, not with the medication, but with a rush of memory.

The sharp taste making the aftertaste of the milk seem a little different.

A little off.

She had tasted that before. Elsie began to shake as the realisation hit her, tempered by disbelief.

Monique had drugged her.

Drugged her, confused her.

Elsie had always known that she could never have wanted to give Ursula away, the loss of her still so visceral in her mind. She had loved her so very much, a tiny embodiment of the forbidden love that she had shared with Josef.

There was no doubt in her mind, the sharp taste in her mouth washing away all the fogginess in her memory, all disbelief.

She had not given Ursula up knowingly and willingly. Never of her own accord.

Monique had taken her baby.

Part 6

Jack

CHAPTER 24

Recovery and Discovery: April 1947

Daniel lowered himself stiffly over the side of his boat and let his toes find purchase in the silty mud of his mooring. As he steadied himself, he reached back and grabbed his crate of fish that he had line-caught today, 'proper fishing' as he liked to think of it and balanced this on his hip as his other hand used his crutch to support him. The fish was a gift. Knowing how much Elsie and Daisy loved sea bass, he had picked out his two best specimens for them to have a fish supper tonight, and he was looking forward to surprising them.

Elsie looked up with a smile when he rapped on the door, and Daisy ran squealing into his arms, screwing up her nose at his fishy overalls.

'You stink,' she said, and Daniel and Elsie laughed.

'It's part of the job description.' Daniel grinned, handing her the crate for her to raise the muslin, revealing two fine, fat fish inside.

'For us?'

'Naturally, ma'am,' he smiled as she threw her arms round him, overalls and all.

Elsie looked at him fondly. 'There's plenty here, enough for three. Would you like to stay for supper?'

And so it happened that, as always in times of need, her dearest friend was with her when the telegram came.

I am home. Stop. I am all right, but weak. Stop. Please collect me from station tomorrow 11 a.m. Stop. Jack. Stop.

***

Daisy looked on worriedly as Daniel made a cup of strong, sweet tea.

'She doesn't like sugar,' she began, but Daniel shushed her, gently.

'Sweet tea is good for shock, and your mummy has had quite a big one today.'

Daisy chewed her lip. 'How come Uncle Jack took this long to write to us? The war was over ages ago.'

'Nearly two whole years,' agreed Daniel. 'I really don't know, love, but I imagine Jack will be telling us a long story tomorrow.'

Daisy wriggled excitedly. She loved long stories, and she had heard so many tales about Uncle Jack, who wasn't an uncle at all, but really half-a-brother.

Elsie smiled and took the tea gratefully. 'Sorry,' she said. 'That gave me quite a turn.'

Then the words burst out. 'How did it take so long? If he was injured, why didn't they send word? I just don't understand. I thought…' She faltered. 'I thought he must be dead.'

Daniel took her hand and clasped it in his own. 'No idea,' he said. 'But drink that, sleep on it, and I'll come round tomorrow at nine. Assuming you want me to come with you?'

Elsie nodded, firmly. 'Yes please, I have a feeling I'm going to need you.'

***

Elsie rose early the next day and dropped the protesting Daisy off at the schoolyard.

'I want to come too, she wailed, but Elsie was having none of it, shushing her firmly.

'Uncle Jack will be very tired from travelling. You can talk to him later after school. I'm sure he'll need a rest after the train journey.'

'Train journey from where?' insisted Daisy, but Elsie shook her head sharply to stop the questions that she couldn't begin to answer. Knowing better than to argue, Daisy turned and flounced up to the school door without any more fuss.

Daniel was waiting by the kitchen door when she returned, and she sat down gratefully while he made them a pot of tea.

'I've checked the Hants and Dorset timetable,' he said. 'If we catch the bus at ten, we'll be nice and early. Then there's one back just after eleven thirty, which we can catch if his train is on time, or we can wait and catch the midday service.'

Elsie nodded; it was so typical of Daniel to sort the practical side out for her that she had not even thought of how to get to the station.

The green bus rolled up promptly at the stop outside the Stanpit Working Men's Club, and after the longest twenty minutes of Elsie's life, they were descending by Christchurch Station and walking on to the little platform.

All they could do now was wait, and Daniel watched as Elsie paced back and forth, back and forth, all the patience that she had shown over the past two years, waiting for the letter that never came while she learnt to mother her sister, all her calm resolve dissolving before his eyes.

And suddenly, the train was clattering to a halt, a burst of steam announcing its arrival. Elsie was still on her feet, although Daniel had been forced to find a seat for his aching leg, and he watched as her face fell.

Only two people got off the train, the guard walking along and slamming the doors behind them. As the whistle blew, Elsie turned to Daniel with confusion and grief all over her face, as they both looked for Jack in vain.

Two people, one a young woman with a wicker basket covered with a checked cloth, the other, an elderly-looking man with a wizened complexion, stooping over a kit bag which he seemed ill-equipped to lift.

An army kit bag.

Elsie gasped, and Daniel leapt to his feet as realisation dawned on them both.

The old man was Jack.

***

It took a long time before Jack could tell them even parts of his story.

He collapsed when they got back to the house, Daniel supporting him with difficulty as he wielded his crutch, and Elsie doing her best to kick open the door while she clutched his bag in shaking hands.

'Japan.'

This was all he could answer when she asked where he had been. Then tears began streaming down his yellowed face, and he held up his hands to ward off more questions.

'I can't talk about it now. I just need a rest.'

Daniel went to put on a kettle while Elsie helped him into the old rocking chair that their father had loved, pulled a blanket over his thin legs, and sat, quietly.

'I know you don't want to talk,' she said eventually. 'But, Jack, you've been, what, lost? For two years. Please. Just tell me where you've been and why it's taken so long.'

And nodding wearily, Jack covered his face with his hands, and slowly, haltingly, began to talk.

The story that he recounted held Daniel and Elsie in its thrall, utterly speechless and struggling to comprehend the horrors he described.

His capture in Malaya (she hadn't even known he'd been there). The Prisoner of War camp, the vermin, the heat and the torture. The relentless cruelty and the hunger, the illness and the suffering of his men all came flooding out on a bitter tide of recrimination.

'When they freed us,' he said, 'when they freed us, the war in the west was over and the war in the east was out of sight, out of mind. We think they wanted to start trading with Japan again, so they shipped us to America, fed us, gave us medicines. I might look bad now, but when I was released, I was really sick. I couldn't eat at all and weighed half this weight. I think they tried to fatten us up before we could come home, so that Japan wouldn't be accountable.' He spat the last word, and the tears ran unchecked, his head finally falling forwards into exhausted slumber.

Elsie piled on another rug over his wasted frame and looked at Daniel to see the horror reflected in his eyes.

'Could you go and fetch Daisy?' she mouthed, and Daniel nodded, relieved to be out in the fresh air and away from what he had just heard.

'Tell her Uncle Jack is sleeping.'

***

It took long months of nursing to help Jack regain some of his strength. His constitution appeared fundamentally weakened, and he struggled to eat, and to keep down, much of the food that Elsie prepared for him.

In the end, she found that he was able to manage white fish, so long as it was simply boiled, not fried, and bit by bit, he began to eat a little more each day. She also realised he couldn't tolerate any of the powdered eggs that were part of their still meagre rations and decided to take matters into her own hands and source him some better food as soon as she could.

Once an idea had formed in Elsie's head, she couldn't let it go. Arising early the next morning, she went down to the shed where her father's fishing gear was still stored. Opening the door wide so that the sunlight could penetrate the dust and cobwebs inside, she stood for a moment, overwhelmed with her memories, both of Dad and of the early days borrowing his gear to go fishing with her new-found friend.

Taking a deep breath, she pushed further inside and began to shift the accumulated gear out of the way, until she finally found what she was looking for.

Her dad's old bike. A bit rusty, but still serviceable, she decided after cleaning and inspecting it in the yard, and although the brakes no longer worked, she decided she would simply drag her feet to stop.

As soon as Daisy was dispatched to school, she set off, pedalling slowly but with dogged determination, in the direction of Holmsley and Mrs Pidgley.

It took her less time than she expected; the miles flying beneath her pedals as her memories guided her to what had been her home for most of the war.

She paused at the top of the track, noting that the sign for the farm had been put back up again now the war was over, creaking as it swung in the light breeze. The smell of the gorse assailed her as she rode the last little stretch of the lane, and a smile broke out as she saw Mrs Pidgley in the doorway of the farm kitchen, staring up the lane to see who should be visiting so unexpectedly.

Some time later, they sat in companionable silence, elbows resting on the scrubbed pine table as they nursed their cups of tea. Mrs Pidgley studied Elsie for a while, then asked tentatively, 'Did you ever find out what happened to her? To Ursula?'

Elsie sighed. 'Not really. I just don't know where she was taken, so I don't know where to start looking. I wish more than anything that I could.'

'But the telegram. You saw that and signed the agreement? You must know who sent it.'

Elsie stared. 'I signed something. But what telegram?'

It was Mrs Pidgley's turn to stare. 'A telegram came for you. It told you about the arrangements and that once you'd signed, that was it.'

'But... how did you know this?'

'I found it in your bedside cabinet. You used to sleep on the left, Monique on the right. It was in your top drawer, tucked under the lining paper.'

Elsie looked straight into her kindly eyes. 'I used to sleep on the right.'

When Elsie left, some hours later, she was nearly back in Mudeford before she realised she'd left the basket of eggs on the table.

***

The telegram had come from Swanage.

Elsie took it to the post office the next day, as soon as she had packed Daisy off to school, and made a simple breakfast for Jack, chiding herself for forgetting the fresh eggs to feed him up with. Unwilling to risk her local post office, where she knew the post mistress well enough by sight, she jumped on the first bus she could to get to the High Street in Christchurch itself.

The lady at the post office eyed her suspiciously when she asked her question, but then became suddenly sympathetic when she read the content.

'I'm not supposed to tell you this, but if you really are Monique, then I suppose it wouldn't do any harm.'

Elsie crossed her fingers behind her back and gave her a tremulous smile.

'Thank you so much.'

After some time checking records, she was given the information she so craved. The telegram has been sent from the post office in Swanage, in the Purbeck Hills over the other side of Poole Harbour. But the tantalising information she truly needed now was still missing – the name and address of the sender.

But after so much anguish and regret, it was something. Elsie clutched the knowledge to her heart as she went to sit in the graveyard of the Priory, needing time to order her thoughts before going back to her role of mother to her half-sister and nurse to her brother, needing to sit and remember that she was also a birth mother who had been unwittingly led into giving up her first-born child. Her thoughts finally overwhelmed her, and she sat down beneath one of the old oaks trees as her tears overflowed.

'Can I help you, child?'

Elsie started at the kindly voice, pushed back her hair, and quickly wiped her face.

The vicar of the parish was standing over her, a friendly and concerned expression on his craggy face, and he smiled at her, gently.

'Let me help you.'

And Elsie realised she did need help, that this was too big for her to cope with today, all alone. He gave her his hand and led her into the church, golden light dappling through the circular window at the top of the aisle and falling on the warm flagstones within.

Over a restorative cup of tea in the verger's office, the vicar listened quietly to her story, one he had heard from many other girls as casualties of war, girls who had lost their loved ones, girls who had made mistakes and felt they needed to atone.

He took the telegram from her shaking hands and sighed at her stricken face.

'I know who this is likely to be from,' he said, finally. 'I know an orphanage run by nuns near Swanage. But you must ask yourself how you will feel if they cannot help you, if they don't know or can't tell you where she was placed for adoption? It's unlikely she's still at the orphanage after all this time. It's been nearly three years, after all.'

Elsie stared at him, trying to calm the wave of excitement forcing the very breath from her chest.

'I don't know,' she replied truthfully. 'But I do feel I have to try.'

And after more tea and conversation, during which she struggled to contain her rising impatience, she finally left with treasure in her pocket.

An address.

***

That evening, she sat down to write her letter. She had meant it to be factual and to the point, but as the candlelight flickered and danced on the kitchen table, her heart overflowed as she began to write, and the words poured forth in a torrent of dark ink on her page.

Tears flowed too, and she was careful to blot the letter as she folded it carefully and sealed the envelope. She knew she did not want to re-read it in the morning, she just had to post it as soon as she could. She couldn't wait a moment longer. In the end, she arose at dawn and walked to the local post office, knowing that the collection would be earlier from there than at the postbox at the end of the road. Now that the letter was written, after all this time and after all this sorrow, all this hope, it had to be posted, and now.

Part 7

Daisy

Chapter 25

Letters and Lies

The reply came so quickly that Elsie was caught completely unawares.

So utterly unaware, in fact, that she never knew it had arrived.

Daisy was playing that morning, unattended and free as the wind in the backyard. Whooping her way around the castles of dried seaweed and sand that she had spent hours making over the past few days, drawbridges drawn, and moats filled, the child was ready for anything life could throw at her.

Except, perhaps, a letter. A letter confirming that she would have to share her mother with another, unlooked for sister.

A sister that would be closer than Daisy was to Elsie, a real daughter, not just a half-sister. A sister that she thought had gone from their lives forever.

After intercepting the postman, Daisy sat with her back against the wall, facing the sea and out of sight of the woman she now knew and loved as her mother.

Her finger pointed out the words as she sounded each one out, syllable by syllable, spelling out her fate.

Second best. Usurped.

She sat, silent and shocked, unable to function. A chill came over her as a cloud blew across the sun, and with a shudder, she focussed on the curly script one last time, before tearing the letter into tiny shreds and letting it fly with the force of her jealous fury and the offshore breeze.

***

A week went by, then a month. Each day, the pain in Elsie's chest hurt a little more, and each day, the guilt in Daisy's grew.

One evening, Daniel came over for dinner, bearing their favourite fish supper wrapped in paper.

'I got a little lucky today.' He smiled. 'Sea bass and a cuttlefish. A proper feast.'

Daisy squealed with excitement and Elsie's heart caught at the sight of Daniel swinging her up into his arms, a sight all the more poignant as she knew he had to struggle to balance once he'd put his crutch down.

His leg still pained him, and Elsie was so proud of the way he had defied his doctors and carried on with his life on the sea. Daniel never knew it, but she still watched for him, checking as she had done as a girl to make sure his boat was home and safely moored up, whatever the time, whatever the weather. She set her world around the tides and lived and breathed them as he did. His world was about current in the Run and the fishing, but since the day they first sailed together and the terrible night of his injury, hers was about Daniel and his safe return.

'Penny for them?' he asked teasingly, and Elsie jumped, flushing to her roots.

'Put her down and let me get cooking.' she said, brightly, determined to dispel her melancholy mood and the strange sensation she had had while watching Daniel scoop Daisy up with such unfettered love.

She turned to the sink and began to unwrap the fish, noting that Daniel had already cleaned and filleted the sea bass, as well as slicing the cuttlefish into manageable chunks. Her thoughts wondered again. Was his thoughtfulness new, or had he always been so caring? She chided herself mentally, remembering what had become their personal words… 'You all right?'

He had always looked out for her, and now, aching for a letter which never came, day after day, she missed his easy touch, his generous hugs. God, she missed physical contact. She shivered and Daniel glanced around.

'Ghost walked over your grave?' he asked gently.

'Something like that,' Elsie replied and turned back to butter the fish in the skillet.

***

Daisy watched the exchange with exasperation.

As far as she was concerned, it was very, very simple.

Daniel loved Elsie. Elsie loved Daniel. What was it about grown-ups that they couldn't see it, when it was surely staring them in the face?

She thought about her friends from school, so many of them, just like her, being brought up by aunties, cousins, big sisters. So few in a normal family, so few fathers to go around. At least in their case, most people hadn't realised that Elsie was not, in fact, her mother, but her half-sister, and she clung onto that as it made her special, a little bit above the rest.

Just imagine if she had a father too.

She sighed, watching the careful, dignified dance that Daniel and Elsie always made around each other in the candle lit kitchen, one cooking, one cleaning, one serving, one laying the table. Never touching, but so close that she could feel the connection that they didn't seem to be able to feel.

Or were too afraid to.

After dinner, her belly full of fresh fish and her heart full of love, she kissed them both good night and took herself up to bed.

Tomorrow, she decided, tomorrow was the day. She wanted, with all her heart, to make Elsie happy and assuage the guilt that was eating her up inside. If she couldn't let Elsie have her real daughter, she could, at least, let her have Daniel.

Tomorrow, she would make them see.

***

In the end, Daisy didn't really need to do anything, except to suggest that Elsie go fishing with Daniel.

Jack was struggling today, and very out of sorts. His stomach had troubled him all night, and Elsie had lost count of the times she had heard him get up and dash outside to the privy. He did not want breakfast and wanted to be 'left in peace.' His eyes met Elsie's troubled ones, and he sighed.

'Sometimes, nobody can help me,' he muttered. 'I just need rest.'

Daisy faced Elsie in the kitchen.

'That fish last night was lovely,' she began. 'And, Mum, you look so tired. Why don't you go and fish with Daniel? I can look after Uncle Jack. He just needs quiet anyway.'

Elsie looked at her little sister with a guilty rush of recognition. She did, indeed, need a break. She just needed to get out, to get away. She could think of nothing better than to sail out to sea with her best, best friend, free as the wind and with the added thrill of catching their supper as fresh as it may be.

Marvelling at the sagacity of a nine-year-old, she caught her up and hugged her tight.

'There're some leftovers in the pantry. Are you all right to fend for yourself and keep an eye on Uncle Jack?'

Daisy rolled her wise eyes. 'Just go.'

***

The wind was gentle and the sea slight, and they made very little headway against the tide once they were out of the Run.

'Well, this is for fun, there's no rush.' Smiled Daniel. 'Let's just get some lines out and relax.'

Elsie laughed. 'Not exactly hunting talk, my friend.'

She cast her rod expertly down tide, then settled herself to wait for a tentative nibble, gently twitching the line invitingly to whoever might take a chance on the tasty bait they had dug earlier.

Daniel grinned to see her in her usual spot and joined her as soon as he had baited his hooks.

'Did you ever hear from Monique?' she asked suddenly, and for a moment, it seemed that a shadow had crossed the sun.

'No, I haven't,' he answered, carefully.

'I got the impression the two of you had become rather close,' she said, annoyed at herself for the blush that was starting to stain her cheeks.

Daniel paused, twitched his line, and settled back. 'We did, actually.' He admitted. 'I was sad to see you two had fallen out, and' – he glanced swiftly sideways then back to his line – 'I did feel sorry for her.'

'I did too, for a while. We were so close while we were working as land girls, but Daniel…' Her voice cracked. 'Daniel, I found out something about her after the war that I can never forgive her for.'

The whole story tumbled out then, between sobs, and Daniel sat aghast at the enormity of what Monique had done.

'But why? Why would she have done such a thing? She knew you'd have had support.'

Elsie drew a shaky breath. 'I think she knew who the father was. Or guessed. And she couldn't live with that.'

Again, Daniel sat silently, unwilling to interrupt.

Finally, Elsie looked him in the eye. 'I never told you because I thought you'd be so angry with me. Monique was angry enough to take Ursula away from me, and she took her because she was Josef's.'

A heartbeat as Daniel's jaw dropped, a stunned silence as the waves lapped around the boat.

'But... how could she possibly have been Josef's?' he countered, the confusion of the missing years written all over his face, and Elsie took a long breath and told him how she had met him again, how it seemed so natural for them to be together. How devastated she had been when he was taken away.

'How could he leave you when he knew you were expecting?' he spat, then saw Elsie's stricken face. 'He didn't know?'

'He didn't know,' she confirmed. 'I was going to meet him and tell him, but they moved all the PoWs away before D-Day and I never found him again. I did look, again and again...'

Her voice broke, and Daniel's arms went around her.

When she had calmed down, he knew what he had to say. Suddenly, everything seemed terribly simple to him under the clear sky on the calm water with this woman he had known since they were children, a lifetime ago, before the war had torn them all apart.

When he told her how they could be a family, with him, Elsie, and Daisy, and have more children of their own if she would like, she saw with the same clarity as he had, that this was their destiny. It took no hesitation at all to say yes.

'But what about Ursula?' she asked finally, at the end of a long and perfect day, their baskets bulging with fish and their hearts full of love.

'We keep looking,' Daniel said firmly. 'We keep looking until we find her.'

***

They were married shortly afterwards, neither wanting a long engagement. Both wanting to be together as soon as they could, the years of being friends suddenly making the need to be together as husband and wife all the more urgent.

Jack gave Elsie away, her heart breaking as she thought of their big, strong father as she held the arm of her broken brother, his frame wasting away and his stoop making him shorter than her now. Still, he walked her proudly and kissed her gallantly as he passed her hand to Daniel, whose face was wreathed in smiles at the sight of his bride. Daisy watching with an excited smile plastered on her face and holding flowers, tears running down Elsie's face as she murmured the ancient words along with the vicar.

The sun shone and the little wedding party walked the short walk back to the cottage together. They had decided to all live at Elsie's, as there was more space than in Daniel's tiny cottage, and as this was rented, it was easier to let it go. Jack had protested at first, feeling he would be in the way, but as the new couple had pointed out, they tended to live in the kitchen and rarely used the front room, so this could easily stay as Jack's bedroom without causing any bother.

Daisy served up lemonade she had made, and they sat outside on the bank by the harbour to eat the tiny sandwiches she had cut up early that morning. The cotton bunting she and Elsie had made out of old bed linen blew in the breeze, and, looking at the wide smile across Elsie's freckled face, Daniel knew he could never feel so happy again.

***

The guilt grew with the secret Daisy held in her heart.

The letter she had destroyed may have been the first, but it was not the last.

She was utterly shocked when another arrived a month later, the distinctive curly writing jumping out at her as soon as she saw it on the doormat. She had scooped it up casually and put the little pile of bills on the kitchen table, slipping this ticking bomb into the pocket across the front of her pinafore without anyone noticing.

She had wanted to throw it away without looking at it, but finally her curiosity won through, and she slit the envelope open after she had gone to bed, her bedside candle flickering and throwing dark shadows across her face as she sat deciphering the writing.

She wanted to know if Elsie had got the first letter. She wanted to know if Elsie had any plans to come to see Ursula reminding her that she had been told she could never see the girl again, although the Mother Superior did acknowledge that Elsie may have been confused and possibly tricked into giving her up for adoption at the time.

She beseeched her to consider that the girl had now been part of another family since 1944, a family who had taken her in when she was five months old and had looked after her as their own until now. A family who had had their own lives torn apart by the war as had she, a family which was now whole and complete with this little girl who had never known another life. A girl who was now three and wanted for nothing.

Daisy turned over and stuffed the letter deep under her mattress, feeling the information burning inside her as surely as if she had lit the paper it was written upon.

From that day onwards, Daisy met the postman at the door.

CHAPTER 26

Ursula's Birthday: June 6, 1955

It was Ursula's eleventh birthday, and they were going to the beach to celebrate.

Her mother had packed a picnic, and her father was carrying it in a big pack on his back as they walked over the dunes to the beach.

She loved Studland beach. The sand swept as far as she could see in every direction, ending at the steam driven chain ferry to Sandbanks to the east, and the hills of the Purbecks to the west. It never took them long to get here from where they lived in Swanage, but they could never come enough to satisfy Ursula.

She was a child of simple pleasures and could spend hours building elaborate sandcastles while humming under her breath. Her mother, Jean, would look on with delight – her wish to have another child to complete their family had never been granted, so she had learnt to accept that Ursula was, in fact, a perfectly self-sufficient only child.

She was quiet and studious, but as soon as they came to the beach for her birthday treat each year, she would run wild, in and out of the water and amusing herself all day with sand and sea until her skin puckered.

After the weekend was over, Jean sat herself at her writing desk and wrote a few words in the postcard they had picked up from the corner shop in Studland village. While her daughter sat by the fire, curled up with her book as usual, she smiled at her and penned a few quiet lines to the sisters.

A lovely weekend, as always, on Studland beach for Ursula's birthday. She is healthy and happy, and I thank you, today and always.

***

Jack was becoming more and more frail, although he never complained. It made no difference what Elsie cooked for him; his constitution never seemed to pick up. His skin was less yellow than when he had first returned, but all these years later, he still seemed sallow, and his eyes were sunken and deep.

Elsie and Daniel often talked about him in the evenings after they had put their youngest to bed, lowering their voices so as not to alarm Daisy.

Iris had been born in the early hours of New Year five years before, and in Elsie's mind she would always mix up the sounds of festivities rolling across the harbour from the nearby pub with the roaring of the aeroplanes as they launched themselves into the sky on D-Day when Ursula had been born. Again and again, the waves of sound seemed to mirror her contractions, but she was unaware of how time was slipping by, and just how many hours she had been in labour. She did not know when Daniel sent Jack to fetch the doctor, dragging him away from his own family celebrations, but she did remember the sharp needle and a terrible, dragging sensation along with a weak cry.

Iris was much stronger than that first cry and was soon busily suckling at her breast despite the forceps marks either side of her downy head, while Elsie sat and wept over that remembered sensation and deep feeling of loss.

The labour had been tough on her, and Daniel wept too when the doctor told him she should not risk having another child.

Daisy was happy to welcome this baby; she had sat on the landing during most of the night, unobserved by her adopted parents and the tired doctor, and was present by the bed when Iris finally made her entrance.

She had put her to bed tonight, and Elsie hugged her gratefully. 'You are so good with her.'

Daisy knew she wanted to talk to Daniel about Jack, who had not managed to get up from his bed at all today, so she quietly excused herself and went upstairs. She was seventeen now and loved looking after her five-year-old sister, never thinking of her as a niece since the day that Daniel had announced that he and Elsie had applied to formally adopt Daisy as their own daughter. The day that, in her mind, they had become one perfect family.

She slipped quietly along the landing and jumped when she realised Jack was standing in the doorway of her room, leaning hard against the door frame. He was holding a bundle of letters against his chest, and she knew what they were before he spoke, her face paling and the sound of her heartbeat roaring in her ears.

'We need to have a little talk, you and I.'

***

She couldn't recall exactly when she had begun to keep them. At first, she had read them with a terrible compulsion and sense of inevitability. She was drawn to them by blood, and it seemed their call couldn't be denied.

Simple tales of another child in another life, quiet stories of sand and sea and a deep, pervasive contentment. A child that wanted for nothing, parents whose lives were fulfilled. A story put together by a faceless nun, who collected these tales from postcards of every picture-perfect family holiday.

They needed nothing, and Daisy decided to give them nothing more than they had already in their perfect little family across the bay.

But she found it harder and harder to destroy the letters. They seemed to call to her, so that she had to keep them close, reading and re-reading them late at night by the guttering light of her candle.

How could this child make Elsie, HER mother, happier? What else did they need to feel complete? Daniel and Elsie were her parents in name and spirit, and Iris was her beloved baby sister. Another girl, sandwiched between them, unneeded filling in a family that she had made her own. A girl who could so easily push her off her perch as eldest daughter, a girl who could truly claim to be Elsie's first born.

The vitriol of jealousy rose in her throat, and she lifted defiant eyes to meet those of her accuser. For one long moment she saw the confusion and disappointment in his eyes, all the questions she had no intention of ever answering.

It was so easy to snatch to the bundle of letters from his prematurely gnarled hands. From there, it only took one little push to make all her troubles disappear.

***

Jack's funeral took place the following week.

The undertakers had taken his broken body from the bottom of the stairs and taken him away while Daniel sat holding Elsie in his arms out on the bank by the water. Daisy had swept Iris up and taken her out, the little girl sobbing with fright and grief. 'I'll take her for a walk, Dad,' she whispered to Daniel who had nodded gratefully and gone to look after his distraught wife, the woman who had done her utmost to nurse her brother back to some kind of health. Trying to find food that he could stomach, trying to help him reconcile his memories, trying to comfort him from his nightmares. A thankless and ultimately hopeless task, Daniel found himself wondering guiltily if the fall might just have put Jack out of the misery nobody could help him fathom.

The pallbearers lifted the narrow coffin with ease, Jack's wasted frame barely causing them any effort.

Elsie found her eyes drawn to it, although in truth, she wanted desperately to look away. Away from the little box that held her brother, her big brother who comforted her during the dark night when their mother left them, who confided his fears about the war to her deep into that other long night. The brother whose love had compelled her to take Daniel and sail across the sea into grave danger to try to rescue him, the brother who had returned to her from the other side of the world, broken in spirit and now in body. Still Jack, always Jack, always her big brother.

The tears rose in her throat and choked her as she whispered her goodbyes.

***

The change in Daisy's behaviour was abrupt and a challenge for them all.

Despite the turbulence to be expected in the teenage years, she had always been a sunny child, and never prey to moodiness. She seemed to delight in looking after Iris, despite their age difference, and the two were almost inseparable.

Until now.

Since the day they lost Jack, she seemed to retreat from the embrace of the family that mourned him, compounding their grief by this new distance she imposed. When Iris climbed onto her lap one evening for her customary story before bed, Elsie was shocked to see Daisy push her away.

'Daisy, that wasn't kind,' she remonstrated sharply, and Iris promptly burst into tears and tried to climb back up again.

Elsie watched in horror as Daisy shoved her away again, more roughly this time.

'I just need to get on with my own studies.' She whirled away from her little sister whose eyes were full of confusion and hurt, pushed past Elsie and ran up the stairs, her feet pounding the floorboards as she ran.

Elsie scooped Iris up and hugged her hard, her eyes meeting Daniel's questioning look as he came in through the back door.

'More trouble?' he asked quietly, and Elsie answered with a nod as her own eyes filled with tears.

'I know she's grieving, but why does she have to be so cruel?' She burst out, then bit her lip as Iris began to sob.

'Story time, sweetheart.' And Iris climbed onto her welcoming lap and a gentle peace was restored in front of the stove in the cosy kitchen.

Upstairs, however, there was no peace. A turmoil of emotions had wracked Daisy since the day of Jack's death, and she paced the floor, night after night, unable to sleep.

Guilt, self-loathing, fear. And relief, blessed relief that her unforgivable secret had stayed buried.

As she laid her head on the pillow that night and closed her eyes, longing for sleep, once again the sound of Jack's body hitting the floor at the bottom of the stairs thudded in her head and sent her back to her nightly vigil, pacing the floor until a lonely dawn silvered the skies.

Part 7

David

Chapter 27

Endings and Beginnings... *Fins et Debuts*

On the other side of a choppy Channel, Monique paused for a moment from her work.

Straightening her back, she sighed with pleasure as she watched the bees working on the honeycomb brimming with dark golden honey, knowing this year would be bountiful.

'*Abeilles*, bees,' she muttered absently, and was rewarded by a snort of laughter behind her. Turning slowly and calmly so as not to disturb the hive, she grinned at the lanky little boy behind her, his unruly blond hair catching the sunlight and his freckles almost lost in his tan.

'Maman, I know all the English words now.'

She laughed at his cheeky face. 'All of them?' she teased.

'All of them,' he replied firmly.

Monique paused and smiled; he was probably right. Just as her mother had done for her, she had fallen into the habit of repeating every word in both languages, and both had slipped naturally off David's tongue since the day he had uttered his first words.

She smiled and held out both hands. 'Let's go back to the house for supper.'

Later that night, she tucked him up in the bed that had been her own, and as always, David asked for a story. The same story he always asked for, the story of his father, the handsome fisherman who had sailed away once upon a time, but whom David very much hoped he might meet some day.

He had stopped saying that last bit, though, as his mother's face would grow sad, and he couldn't bear that. Enough to hear the stories of the sailor who had rescued Maman and taken her back to her beloved France, a hero of the salt seas.

When his little head had dropped back on the pillow, Monique stood for a while in the doorway, listening to his deep, even breathing.

She had never married but had returned to the farm to find Solange mourning her husband who had died in the war, and soon the two women became as close as before, pooling their resources to keep both farms afloat. The older woman was more than happy to help Monique get the farm up and running again and re-establish the bees, while in return, Monique cared for her and helped her with the heavy work she could no longer manage.

Solange had known Monique was pregnant almost before she did herself. She saw her weariness and her sickness, and one morning, just as Monique had once done for Elsie, she asked her to come and walk with her, and so they began to talk.

Solange talked of the natural rhythms of the farm and country life as they walked, and Monique smiled gratefully, knowing that Solange had realised and was not judging her. Nor did she ask whose it was, but Monique told her without shame, the story of her return to France and the passion suddenly flaring with an old friend, fuelled by the intensity of the moment, a homecoming at the end of the war that had seized and shaped all their lives.

A moment of sudden unlooked-for passion that filled her with love when she looked back. Love and gratitude, but no regrets. With the growth of the child within, she understood that they had shared a moment in time, but that they were not destined to be together. After all she'd been through this didn't matter to Monique. She was simply grateful to be home, nurturing a child to be born in the land of her own birth, in the place that she had always called home.

Yet as the years went by, Monique was troubled more and more by what she had once done to Elsie.

She had judged her. She had arranged for her baby to be adopted without her knowledge or consent, all for the sin of sleeping with the enemy. How different was it to her own sin, sleeping with a friend with whom she had no intention of sharing her life?

Her memory touched on the night in the barn when the Germans came for her, and her mind swung full circle. Surely these beasts should not ever father children, soiling everything they touched. And again, relentlessly, her mind circled back to

Josef, kind, gentle Josef, who had almost certainly saved her life by taking her exhausted hand and running with her into the sea. Josef, whom she knew, in her more honest moments, to be a good man, and whom her friend had loved so very much.

Her mind spinning, she found sleep the only way she knew how. Creeping quietly into David's bed, she snuggled up alongside his hot little body and breathed the scent of his hair until her own troubled thoughts slipped into dreams.

***

As the day of David's tenth birthday dawned, the delicious smell of baking wafted upstairs and woke him, sending him clattering down to the kitchen in excitement.

Just as he had expected, Monique and Solange were waiting for him, the early morning sun slanting through the shutters onto the table, where his birthday breakfast awaited him.

Cramming his mouth with pastry, he whirled around and hugged his mother tightly, not noticing that she grimaced with pain just as he released her from his sturdy grip.

But Solange noticed, and not for the first time.

After David had been dispatched to play in the fields with his friends, Solange poured coffee for them both and sat down firmly, her hands clasped together on the kitchen table.

Monique glanced at her with surprise.

'Aren't you going to market today?'

Usually, Solange headed off early on Saturdays to take their eggs and honey to the local town market, and Monique would settle down to the milking.

'Sit down,' Solange said quietly, and Monique sat abruptly, a tug of dread at her heart.

'What is it? Are you ill?' she asked fearfully.

'No, child, I am not ill. But, Monique, I believe that you are.'

Monique stared.

'I am perfectly well.' She protested, and was shocked to see Solange shaking her head, and worse, tears starting in her eyes.

'I've heard you coughing, and I see you are in pain when you lift or when David hugs you,' she stated simply. 'You must see a doctor, Monique, and you must see one soon.'

***

As Solange had feared, it was confirmed that Monique was suffering from tuberculosis, just like her mother before her.

The disease was active in her lungs and spine, and she had begun to wake at night, sweating with pain and hauling herself upright to try to cough up the fluid that was choking her.

Monique had known deep inside what she had before the doctor uttered the words, but even so, the confirmation felt like a shock. She had been feeling so fit and strong, but now she realised that symptoms had been creeping up on her bit by bit and the penny had dropped too late.

'What about my son? Will he catch it too?'

The doctor looked at her sympathetically.

'We are going to treat you with the most modern techniques we have to hand. But yes, he could catch it. Is there anyone who could help you look after him? Any way you could reduce your physical contact with him until we see if the medication is working?'

'If.' Monique's heart contracted. Barely able to stop herself from sobbing aloud, she nodded, then excused herself, aware of the doctor's kindly eyes following her as she left the building.

Not have physical contact with David? Child of her blood, her only son?

Solange saw the steps that told her that her friend was finally broken. The woman she had nurtured as a child and rescued as a young woman, whom she had admired and applauded on her return to her home after the war. A woman who had had every reason to give up and crumble, Solange had watched her rebuild her farm and her old ways at the same time as building a new life as a mother.

Monique had never once cracked or complained. She had laughed off her constant bee stings, shrugged at her bruised feet from careless moments with her cows. She had single-handedly raised David at the same time as recreating her cottage industry of honey and beeswax, as well as caring for an ever-increasing dairy herd.

But this time, this time, was different. This news had knocked her to the ground and left her there, bleeding.

Solange went to the gate to meet her, the sympathy and understanding in her eyes breaking down the last reserve Monique could have mustered.

'David,' she managed, before the sobs took the last of her breath away, and, wordless, Solange knew what she was trying to say.

'I will care for him.'

It only took that to release Monique, and from that point forth, her fate became an inevitable slide towards a final release. The end of her fight for herself, but not the end of her fight for David.

In her last few weeks, the doctor withdrew the medication as it was not helping her at all and was making her sicker. At this point, she asked Solange to bring David to her to explain what would happen next.

In the calm candlelight of her bedroom, Monique took her child into the crook of her withered arm and talked. Talked like she had never talked before. She told him all the stories she had withheld, about where he came from, the reason he knew so many English words. The reason she had never suggested he meet his father, a good man but not hers to share. The path that he must choose for his future. Solange protested.

'I can care for him.'

But Monique insisted. 'He must know, and he must have the choice.'

David, his young face awash with shock, with anger and with fear, and finally succumbing to what he knew would be an endless grief.

***

When the sun set that evening, Solange found David sitting behind the barn, watching the light slip below the trees on the horizon.

He was dry eyed now, the tears from the funeral in the church now replaced by a cold, hollow feeling in his chest.

He looked up as Solange came around the end of the barn and smiled weakly.

'Sorry. I shouldn't have run off like that.'

Solange felt her heart break a little more. 'You don't need to be sorry. I knew where you'd be, and today of all days, I wasn't expecting you to feel like talking.'

David reached out and squeezed her hand. 'Actually, I do.'

He took a deep breath. 'I would like to meet my dad. I don't know if I want to stay there, but I'd like to meet him, at least.'

Solange bit back her tears and nodded. 'I have an address for you. Maman wanted me to keep it until you asked. Shall we write a letter together? You know enough English words—'

'Actually, all of them,' he interrupted, and they both laughed, the first laughter in this long, long day, and the world seemed a little brighter.

***

Daisy swung through the door that afternoon and stopped dead.

Something was different, something fundamentally altered.

They were all there, but their focus had shifted. Indeed, none of them looked up as she pushed the door to.

'What is it?' she asked afraid.

Elsie visibly shook herself, twisted to meet her eye.

'We have had a letter. A letter from an old friend. To be honest, it's given us quite a shock.'

Daisy went cold inside.

Fearing the answer, not wanting to know. 'A letter? But who from?'

The answer, when it came, surprised and relieved her.

Not from Swanage. From France.

But the next few words hit her from a different angle, different but just as hard.

'It seems I have a son.' Daniel spoke carefully, but she could hear the quiet elation he was doing his best to control. 'I know it wasn't exactly planned, or really the right thing, but it seems I have a son in France. A son who has just lost his mother, an old friend of ours…'

Daisy saw Elsie's visage darken momentarily.

'An old friend,' Daniel repeated. 'And my boy wants to meet me. And it seems he might need a home.'

***

Daisy lay in her bed, her mind spinning.

A son. Daniel's own blood.

And with Iris, a daughter to both Daniel and Elsie, the woman she had increasingly thought of as her own mother over the years, they had their perfect little family.

The futility of trying to hide her knowledge of Ursula's whereabouts over the years hit her, finally, and with it, the guilt of what she had done to Jack.

She swung her legs over the edge of the bed, sat with her feet on the cold wooden boards. Her stomach was churning, and her heart beating fast.

They could have it all.

Daniel could have his son, this David, who had appeared from nowhere. He and Elsie already had their own daughter, Iris. And she had the power within her to give Elsie back her first-born daughter, Ursula.

But what would that make of her, the twenty-year-old cuckoo in their nest?

She bent over, trying to steady the pain building in her stomach, the pain that had festered since the day Jack had fallen down the stairs. Been pushed.

And there it was. It hit her viscerally, and she doubled up over the cramps, as she had over and over again since that dreadful night, that split-second decision that had, ever since, all the time in the world to destroy her.

She had killed her own half-brother. She had done it to stop Elsie finding out about her baby girl, a child who had wrongfully been taken from her.

Not only did she have no real place in this family – a half-sister? An adoptee? She was a killer and a home-breaker.

There was no other way of looking at it.

Once she had a hold of the cramps, she took her pen, and wrote the lines that would change the world of the people who had taken her in and cared for her forever.

Then, very carefully, she made her bed for the last time and walked out into the night.

***

Elsie would never quite remember the sequence of those next terrible days.

Walking into Daisy's room, to find the bed empty and unslept in.

Seeing the note, neatly tucked under a corner of the pillow so that it was secure but plainly visible.

Reading it and falling to her knees on the hard boards, the shock leaching the strength from her.

Daniel rushing upstairs when he heard the crash as she fell, scooping her up and lying her down on the bed, taking in her ashen face and the letter clutched to her breast.

A sharp breath in. 'Daisy has gone. And Ursula is in Swanage.'

***

The police were told but weren't very interested. As far as they were concerned, a young woman had legitimately left home and was, therefore, not missing.

And while her heart twisted in grief over where Daisy might be, whether she was cold and hungry and alone, Elsie couldn't help her mind turning towards Swanage, towards the search for her own firstborn which she had given up before in the face of the apparent silence from her enquiries.

And across the channel, Solange helped David to pack for his journey, not knowing whether this would be the briefest of an 'au revoir,' or an intolerable 'adieu.'

And the next week, the weather whipped up and tides became enormous surges of power, making the Run unnavigable for the fishermen of Christchurch who couldn't fight or ride those currents safely, so used the time to sit on the town quay, mending nets, fashioning repairs, and servicing their boats.

And it was those same men who went to tell Daniel and Elsie when the body was washed ashore.

Chapter 28

Josef's Search

A world away, a gaunt, blond man straightened his shoulders and strode through the heavy wooden doors and into his office. His secretary smiled at him and handed him a sheaf of opened mail, and he sat down at his desk and began to sort through his paperwork.

Josef had always thought he would follow his father into teaching history, but when he was returned to Germany after the war, he found that this no longer held any interest for him.

The plight that he found his mother in had shocked him to the core, and into action.

Frieda was starving. Her face was deeply lined, and she was stooped, appearing at least twenty years older than her true age. She had a permanent limp - she had broken her ankle one evening going out to the shelter in the street, and because of the lack of vitamins in her terrible diet, the bones had refused to knit properly. He could hardly bear to look at the thickened bone protruding above the ankle boot she had cut apart to force over her foot, and the pain she was suffering silently broke his heart.

The day that he had returned to his home, they had sat and wept in each other's arms, scarcely believing the changes they could see in one another.

And then, with his customary determination and focus, Josef began to try to change things for the better for his mother and his beaten countrymen.

Five long years later, he had qualified from the university where his father had one taught and devoted his time to tracking and reuniting families torn apart by the war.

His chosen line of work was busy – far busier than he would ever have believed.

PoWs like himself, returning to a bombed-out street and the family missing, 'no forwarding address.' Sons and husbands who never came home. Telegrams with the stark words 'missing in action' which were never resolved. Families which were split up and children evacuated to safer places, children who then disappeared.

Josef devoted his early work to forging links with organisations such as the Red Cross and the Salvation Army, and now he spent his days sending letters out into the world to search, discover and reunite, or frequently, to help someone find closure by finding that their loved ones had died.

He squinted at the letter in front of him and paused, pitching the bridge of his nose hard.

The name 'Elsa' had jumped out at him, and the reminder of her name, of Elsie, had thrown him momentarily. His secretary glanced up at him in concern, but he shook his head sharply and she knew better than to interrupt his thoughts.

He wondered, as he had done over and over again, whether he should try to find her, whether she still lived in the little cottage by the harbour. But every time, he remembered Daniel, knowing that he had loved her first, and that they might have found a happiness that was not his to disturb.

Little did he know how much Elsie needed him now, needed his skills to find their daughter – the daughter that he had never known existed. The daughter that she had lost and almost found, a daughter who seemed to slip away again every time she seemed close.

For Elsie had written to the address that Daisy had left her, only to find that the nun who had written to her periodically for all those years had died, and that nobody else was able or willing to help her.

All she knew was that Ursula loved to go to the beach on her birthday, that long stretch of spare beauty that was Studland. And she knew that she would scour those sands herself every June 6 for the rest of her days.

And at the end of another day of tracking family members down, some with joy but more with grief, Josef shut the door to his office and walked out onto the street, never knowing that the woman he had loved needed him now, but not for his love, but for his skills in finding the daughter he never knew they had once had together, and then lost.

Part 8

The Family Tree

CHAPTER 29

Studland: 2010

The shrill ringing of the telephone made Iris jump. She had been working at her desk in her little study and spent a few panicky moments running through to the kitchen to try to locate the phone. Why the kids couldn't put just it back on the handset was beyond her, and she had to take a breath and moderate her tone to avoid snapping 'hello' when she finally managed to answer the call.

It was David, and Iris smiled as she settled herself in to her favourite chair for what she assumed would be one of their long cosy chats.

But what she heard made her sit up sharply, almost knocking her tea over with her elbow.

Over the next half an hour, David described how his daughter, Emma, had begun researching their family tree as a school project. She had begun with a genealogy website and then branched off into her own social media to try to speed up a process that she had been finding tedious.

And she had found a name that might possibly be the answer to her grandmother's prayers.

A name that was somewhat unusual at the time, a child of German and English descent, a child who had been given up for adoption during the latter part of 1944.

'Emma thinks she's found Ursula.'

***

Iris waited impatiently for her mother to arrive home. Her son, Thomas, was puzzled by her clear agitation, but she couldn't bring herself to tell him the news until she had spoken to her first.

When Elsie nudged the kitchen door open with her hip, her pure silver hair catching the light as she backed in with her faithful shopping trolley loaded down with fruit and veg from the market, she stared in alarm at her daughter, who had gone quite pale at the enormity of what she was about to impart.

'Whatever is it?'

'Mum, sit down. It's good news.'

***

The ensuing days were an ordeal for them all.

Although it seemed that Emma had indeed found Ursula, she had sent her a message and there had yet to be a response. Looking at her Facebook profile, which was public and viewable by all and sundry, she clearly was not a regular user, with the last post being almost a year ago.

The days dragged endlessly, ironically towards the date where they would habitually go and walk the beach in Studland as a family, eyes sweeping the sands, searching for a face none of them could know. The trip had begun with Daniel and Elsie so many years before, and had become part of the extended family tradition, all of them, every year come what may, searching the sands on the anniversary of D-Day.

Then David, his wife, Sarah and Emma arrived for the ritual weekend, and they all sat and poured over the Facebook entries under the name of Ursula Downing.

It was Thomas who spotted it in the end.

A single snapshot, a tiny moment in time that gave Elsie everything she needed to find her daughter. A view that she had known for many years but had bypassed thoughtlessly in her quest to walk the beach itself.

Shell Bay. The little seafood restaurant, not facing the open sea, but on the harbour side, a gentler view across to Brownsea Island and the calm beauty of Poole Harbour itself. A smiling face, a woman surrounded by two young women who must be her daughters, and Elsie's heart leapt within her breast as she saw what must be two more grandchildren of her own.

'She has her birthday lunch at Shell Bay,' said Tom. 'We must have walked past her a thousand times…'

'There's no point in waiting for a reply,' said Emma firmly. 'She'll be there. She'll be there in two days from now.'

Elsie looked at Iris, then at David. 'I just wish your father could be here too,' she said, her eyes filling with ready tears.' I would have loved us to have been all together for this.'

Yet that night, as she laid down on her side of the double bed, she had shared for so many years with the man who had made her his wife, the man who had brought up their family with her, shoulder to shoulder, she let her mind drift back to another time. A guilty start as she realised that, just maybe, this might be easier without her late husband, a man whose life had been made complete by their daughter and the arrival of his own son.

A husband who, while faithful and understanding, had never quite fathomed her unconditional love for Josef, a man who could never have been her enemy and a man who had left the war to ensure that he remained a man of peace.

When Daniel had died, Elsie had mourned him fiercely, the loss of her husband quite as bad as the loss of her lifelong friend. The friend who had given her a purpose, who had taught her to fish and to sail, the man who had brought her father back to himself in the very act of rescuing him from the sea he so feared.

Elsie rolled over onto her back and stared, dry eyed at the ceiling, the reflected light from the water outside flickering in tiny ripples across her bedroom.

This June 6 must be all about her, and all about Ursula. She needed to explain, needed her eldest daughter to know that she had not given her away, would never have knowingly or willingly given her up.

She passed a thought for Daisy too, although this would always be tinged with guilt and anger. She had never understood why Daisy had been so afraid of Ursula tipping her from the nest like a cuckoo, why she did not see that she was as much a part of the family as Daniel and Monique's child was.

Why – Elsie's mind clouded in old grief – why she had pushed Jack to his death rather than allow the truth to come out. Why she felt that she was better off dead than finding her way through with her growing family, a family, like so many after the war, made up of half-siblings, of nieces and nephews, of cousins and of new life.

Of hope.

Why so many years had slipped by since losing her daughter and the chance of finding her again, so near and yet so far from home.

Elsie rolled again, trying to ease the stiffness in her joints and covering her face with her blankets in the hope of finding sleep before dawn.

***

The day had dawned dry and bright, and a few tourists stood by and watched idly as the little family walked down the ramp.

The old lady paused and reached out for her grandchildren with her wizened hands, and they both reached to steady her as they stepped over the divide to leave the chain ferry.

Every year the same, her rheumy old eyes ignoring the view but sweeping the beach, hardening to gimlets as she focussed on the dog walkers and the day trippers.

Every year since Daisy had died for Elsie, every year since they were born for them.

But this year was different.

This year they understood why.

And this year would be an end to it.

Turning away from her annual pilgrimage along the sands of Studland Bay, the old lady set a determined pace along the road, weaving her way imperiously between the cars queuing to take the ferry they had just left.

The little building that was Shell Bay was on her right, and she stopped, staring at the open door.

**

She would always remember it afterwards in the passage of heartbeats.

Beat.

When she walked through the door, closely followed by the family that had become hers alone, she saw the woman sitting by the window, her brown hair streaked with white but with curls as unruly as her own had always been.

Beat.

The woman looked up, puzzled, as Elsie stopped in her tracks, unable to take any more steps but equally unable to tear her gaze away.

Beat.

'Can I help you?' she asked then stared in her own turn, the shock of recognition stamped upon her face.

Beat.

And a lost lifetime was found again as mother and daughter stepped together and wrapped their arms around one another, the first contact since those hazy days of starfish hands, of hot milky skin, of baby smiles and midnight feeds, of the deepest love and the most heart-rending loss.

Beat.

***

Ursula had two daughters, and the next hour was spent in incredulous talk when they both arrived together to celebrate their mother's birthday.

When Elsie asked about a husband, her face contracted with grief.

'He died last year. I so wish you could have met him.'

And as Elsie acknowledged her daughter's grief, Ursula unveiled a secret of her own.

After she had lost her husband, she had decided to try to track down her own family. The fact that Monique had signed her own name on some of the papers had made it impossible for her to find

Elsie, but because the father's name was on some of the remaining paperwork which she found after her adoptive mother died, she knew her father's name.

And she had tracked him down, over the years and across the borders into Germany, but – and Elsie wept anew - she had been too late.

Josef had died five years ago. He had never married, not had any other children. The woman whom Ursula discovered had once worked for him had a few personal keepsakes and asked if she would like her to post them to England, and Ursula had gladly accepted.

Wrapped up in a little scrap of velvet was a shell, which she had found in the breast pocket of the jacket he always wore, and which Ursula had carried with her ever since. A shell a desperate girl had once given him on the day that he went to give himself up to the English police. The shell that Elsie had given him to try to sustain his hope through the rest of the war, and a shell that he had kept close to his heart for the rest of his life.

Elsie reached out a shaking hand and took it, pressed it against her ear and listened to the sound of the sea as the tears rolled silently down her face.

Mother and daughter, eyes locked, heartbeat to heartbeat. Just as it always had been. Just as it always should have been.

'I never got to meet him,' said Ursula, quietly. 'But I know he must have loved you so much. I'm just so glad that you found me.'

'He didn't know about you, you know.' Ursula went still as Elsie began to speak. 'I never got a chance to tell him. But you were wanted and loved from the moment I knew about you.'

'So why…?'

David stepped in. 'That's a very, very long story.'

Elsie held out her hands again to her daughter across the table, glanced out at the silver water of the harbour and felt the depth of her memories flooding in with the rising tide. She took a firm breath and smiled around at her family, old and new.

'And now we have all the time in the world to tell it.'

ACKNOWLEDGEMENTS

First, to my husband and kids, for your enthusiastic encouragement at every step of the way.

Second, an enormous thank you to Emma Mitchell of Creating Perfection, editor extraordinaire. Not only have you dragged me out of the darkness and encouraged me to write for your amazing *Help4Heroes* publications, but you gave me invaluable advice and support with my first novel and have been there for me once again editing this new offering and getting it publication ready.

A huge hug to Kelly Lacey of Love Book Tours, for being a friend and advisor.

Grateful thanks to Amanda Horan of Let's Get Booked for the amazing cover design – thank you for persevering with my whims.

Much appreciation to Howard Cutler, of Christchurch History in Pictures, for your invaluable advice on local sea defences of WW2, the airfields, and the bus services.

To Tom, my wonderful son, for saving the day with a last minute edit upload issue – it always amazes me that you Know Stuff!

And finally, a special mention to my beautiful daughter, Emma. You modelled for the cover of *Walking Wounded* when you were nine, and now, at the age of sixteen, you have graced the cover of *Beyond Time and Tide*. You caught the mood so beautifully, and I'll never forget the moment we both looked at the photo and knew it was *The One*.

Printed in Great Britain
by Amazon